Michael Perry Allen

50 Million Reason

Michael Perry Allen

LCCN: TXu-2-464-734

ISBN: 979-8-218-59496-1

Book cover designs by CC

Destiny fills our souls, you either lead, follow or just get out of the way.

I am not a doctor, nor am I an educated scientific philosopher.

I am just a guy.

Introduction

This book represents a story I needed to tell. The thoughts that once floated endlessly in my head are now expressed in the pages that follow. This novel will provide an informal nonscientific outlook of how the mind thinks, then acts on those thoughts of creativity. The fictional story provides laughter and a few tears. Simple observations into understanding how each of us ponder questions within our minds. No one can hear your own thoughts, and no one can read your mind while you are engaged in self-thinking. You can only hear yourself.

The fictional characters chosen in this novel have no bearing on actual people, I personally know any reference to actual people are coincidental at best. It does contain actual places across the globe I have personally experienced on my travels.

A process we humans use to digest information begins our cognitive thinking. You will read in detail how it has worked for me. It is this initial thinking before we decide to create with our hands what we first envision. How a healthy normal mind can contribute to an individual's success or failure.

We all seek answers to questions that either trouble us or inspire our path in life. These thoughts begin inside all of our minds as we deliberate with ourselves in how it guides us to a conclusion with some philosophy of life mixed with a fictional story.

TABLE OF CONTENTS

50 Million Reason

I am just a guy who authored a book.

Michael Perry Allen

It Is in Your Head.

Looking up at an architectural masterpiece captures the creative idea that once existed only in someone's mind.

A design begins as a dream that eventually develops into reality.

All modern-day classic or gothic building designs begin as a thought floating around in the portion of the brain that stores a person's memory. The thought is always there.

"In the back of the mind, they say."

These thoughts frequently re-occur and fade away, forgotten. Then without any reasoning, you become engaged with them again.

The memories are mostly of personnel experiences from an encounter with someone. A friend, stranger, or family member. So very often, it is about a loved one. A recent exchange with a stranger or the passing of a close family member or a friend. It is these experiences that create our memory. Often enough our thoughts are most vulnerable to emotional feelings. Especially if the encounter was emotionally draining to the individual.

The mind can recall our memories during sleep, as in a dream. You remember conversations or envision a new conversation with words you failed to select during the real time and the place the event took place. This created the memory for further deliberation as the situation required further analysis. Simply put you need to find and accept the conclusion to the encounter before you can erase the memory.

Creativity comes to a person's internal thoughts while engaged in physical activity. This period of time is a silent space when you are least distracted. More so when you are alone, removed from the direct contact of personnel conversation with another person.

You could be showering, washing a car, mowing the grass, listening to music, or sitting alone at a bar sipping your favorite scotch. Your mind slips into self-isolation mode. It will begin insulating itself from the reality of noise or movement around you.

When a person begins this transition into his or her mind, they experience a euphoric like trance. The mind steps back from its current situation of movement or current activity for a moment, then, for reasons unknown, you become one with yourself.

You slip into a different dimension of cognitive thinking. The physical activity you are engaged in continues as if you selected, autopilot. You could be hiking a trail, walking a dog, or driving a car on an interstate, you become unaware of the time and distance you have traveled. We have all been there. The physical activity continues although unaware of motion or sound, you exist within a personal space with a total loss of self-awareness.

As you become internally focused. Your mind selects a memory for recall.

Quite often of a loved one, in the present or past tense, a project you need to begin or complete. You deliberate with yourself, inside the small space of your brain. Each time you begin, a piece of the puzzle comes together to form your conclusion. There is no audible sound wave from your vocal cords. Although you hear each piece of a conversation you had with someone. A lie, from a cheating lover captures your thoughts forever.

Although you can hear your own words as you work through the details with precision and accuracy. Each time you read a sentence in a book you hear words in your head. You conduct an orchestra of opinions to reach a balance of what it is you may be designing or what is troubling you.

During this sequence, normal sounds enter your ears but do not register. You enter an unexplainable dimension of time, oblivious to everything known to exist. These thoughts are mere templets of the final process of a realistic design, staying put until you decide to scribble them on a napkin.

Great men-built city after city, artists carved magnificent sculptures, others brush their thoughts with magnificent creativity with paint on a canvas for the world to admire. There is not a single item we use personally, commercially, or industrially, that had not come from the mind of an individual who first had a vision that would change our lives or the world.

Forever.

Robert Killings Jr.

While sitting at his private club, Robert Killings Jr. did just that. He designed a magnificent office building in his mind.

Robert recalled his memory repeatedly as he sat alone in a packed bar with noise and commotion around him. It was the best place for Robeert to enter the silent zone he cherished while sitting alone, sipping his scotch. waiting for the thoughts of his masterpiece to begin filling his mind.

When he knew he was fully engaged in his creative mindset, he began to scribble what his mind envisioned on to a cocktail napkin.

The new Killings insurance LLC. building would be a marvelous achievement to his successful career.

Robert Killings Jr. never left the napkins behind. always stuffing them in the pockets of his trousers, his business suit, or occasionally in his wallet alongside a few C-notes that rarely became exposed.

Robert Killings was an only child. Nurtured by devoted parents to excel and succeed with his life after their passing. His parents granted him access to every piece of literature available.

His mother would drive him to the library at an early age, watching over him and his selection of material for reading. The Killings acquired professional tutors with advanced teaching techniques to further his skills that would enhance and ensure his ability to develop an intellect far superior to his peers at any age level.

Thus, Robert began planning at an early age to create what would become the perfect career as a major player in the insurance industry.

Graduating from college he decides to approach success in an alternative manner. Instead of being handed a comfortable position at his father's company. He began applying to several of his father's competitor companies first as an intern to gain wisdom and experience that a college degree could never provide.

This knowledge would prove vital when the time came to step into the old man's shoes, or when his father decided to pass the torch.

Not wanting to be viewed by his peers or future employees as an entrepreneur gifted the reins of daddy's business he never worked a day to deserve it. He always feared no one would respect his decisions as a leader and CEO of anything much less his father's business.

Being handed the silver spoon was not in his grand scheme. The process of climbing to the top of a corporate ladder needed to be earned. His ideal status would be to acquire enough peer respect while on the journey to the top of that ladder was a major part of the equation.

Planning his career in separate stages. Each step was a calculated game of chess. No move was to be made by chance; the decisions were decisive as they were precise. Luck has no place in history.

"A pawn is always a pawn, but a true leader is a king."

His father always had a quote for success.

"Do not wet the rungs of the ladder as you climb to the top. Because if you do. You will most always slip and fall back down."

Several years working as an understudy insurance claims adjuster proved beneficial in learning the many ways clients prepare brilliant stories full of fraudulent lies to collect money. Especially the ones listed as a beneficiary in insurance policies.

By the time he was ready to step up on another rung on the ladder, Robert had become a seasoned veteran in the multitude of deceptive tactics people use. It was impossible for anyone to fool him. There were many promotions as his career progressed. Robert just naturally excelled in every position offered to him.

Aside from the rigors of demanding work. Robert loved flying airplanes and pursued aviation as a hobby at an early age. Figuring if he was going to learn aviation, he needed a 'Top Gun' type flight instructor. Shying away from a local aviation weekend fly school.

He wanted to learn how to fly from a seasoned veteran. An instructor with combat flying experience. Robert visited the local piper airport outside of New York to acquire recommendations on the best of the best.

Entering the lobby, he sought out the young attendant at the check-in counter. Robert introduced himself and then relayed his reasoning to learn to fly from one of the best.

The attendant looked at Robert with a grin and pointed across the lobby at a small four-foot-eight-inch stubby gentleman staring out the window at an old vintage plane that had now landing.

Robert could see he was a short man with some age, a grey beard, long sideburns, brandishing the sixties hippie attire with a ponytail down his back, neatly secured with rubber bands.

"That's the guy you want" uttered the young attendant.

"What is his name?" Robert asked,

"I am not sure but, everyone just calls him, "SPARKY."

"Ok, I guess I can learn why later. For now, I will go introduce myself."

Robert approached the man with caution.

Sensing someone was standing to his left side. Sparky slowly turned away from the window to look up at Robert.

Robert extended his hand to introduce himself.

Exchanging pleasantries, Sparky asked the big question.

"What can I assist you with Mr. Killings?

Robert toned down the hierarchy by informing Sparky they should begin this friendship with first name recognition. It was at that moment ole "Sparky" and Robert, bonded as friends. After a lengthy discussion of requirements and pricing they shook hands again to seal the deal.

Robert had officially signed up for flight school.

Hours and weeks of classroom with the book instruction now completed. Robert admired Sparky's diligence with a regimental military approach to learning professional flying skills.

Robert's day had come. It was time to solo on his own.

Sparky informed Robert.

"This is your big day. I will be on the ground with a handheld radio critiquing your skills to take off and land on your own If I say abort landing. You know what to do. I will not have time to discuss why. Do not think, do not ask why, just ABORT the landing."

"Got it.' Replied Robert.

Robert completed the required take-off and landings with a couple touch and goes mixed in. Finally taxing the plane in front of the hanger. Robert was ready for the test results.

"Excellent flying Robert, you are a natural aviator, all that is left at this point is for me to sign off and you are officially a pilot."

"Sparky, I have one last question for you?"

"What would that be Robert?"

"I never asked before and honestly. I do not mind if you do not want to tell me, but how did you acquire the nickname, Sparky?"

"Most people ask right away. They were more concerned or inquisitive than you. I figured you just did not seem to care to know the answer to that question."

"It was a long time ago; I landed a wounded Warthog on a carrier. The front landing gear was damaged by small arms fire and would not extend into the lock position. I was lucky the cable stopped the plane, with a lot of sparks but no fire. After the incident, and from then on, everyone called me, Sparky."

"Thank you for your service, Sparky, I am sure the nickname was well deserved," replied Robert.

Robert's weekends were now filled with adventurous destination flights to places he had never been to before. So many places he desired to explore. A new state, a historical monument, a town that required his discovery. He had to find the right place if his future dream were to work out.

Driving a car was not much of an option for Robert beyond a one-hundred-mile radius. Flying to a destination was much quicker, allowing more time for exploration and discovery. Once he landed at a destination, only then would he even consider the need for a vehicle to drive himself around. He could not stand cab drivers as he likened them to a rickshaw with a motor and wheels.

Robert was on a mission to find a location that would someday be suitable for relocating Killings Insurance LLC.

His Father was aging and rightfully should retire. Although good old dad had the idea, he was still young enough to get up every morning and head to work. From the old school everyone joked. It is what a man did, back in his days.

Robert flew his newly acquired Cessna single engine to more places in a year than most people see in a lifetime. Every location was checked out thoroughly.

Creating an excel spread sheet with a list of requirements he felt the city he chose should have for his employees. Should they agree to transfer with him? The area of choice must sufficiently support hiring new talented individuals without the need for an outside search using a recruiter.

A map of the United States hung on the wall of his penthouse apartment in New York city. The map now covered with penciled notepads, everywhere within the boundaries of the closest States he had traveled too already. A red X over the state signified that the State did not meet its requirements.

Not enough infrastructure for traveling or economic support for the business, either from the local or state government, then the location would be ruled out. While other States were still in the running. He placed the same sticky pads on those with a note for future reference. Yellow for further consideration at the top of his list and a red sticky note for future reference but not at the top of the list. This red notepad was just before receiving the big red X.

Robert decided not to leave New York this weekend. He stepped into the kitchen to grab his morning coffee from an old-style percolator his father gave him as a birthday present years before. Pouring his first cup, he stepped back into the bedroom. Blowing on the coffee to cool it before taking his first sip, his mind began to think.

"My father is so smart. This is the best way to brew coffee."

Looking out the bedroom window of his penthouse with coffee in hand. Robert watched one of the last snows of the winter blanket the streets below him. There were no trees in sight, just buildings. Buildings everywhere he looked.

He could not help but think.

"I have to find a better place to work, where the scenery is more spectacular than this city of concrete, steel and glass."

One moment he is in the bedroom, a moment later Rober left the bedroom and was standing in the living room staring at the Map pinned to the wall.

The map was a little out of place and did not fit in with its décor of the penthouse decor. It did not bother him to pin it up in the living room, he was a bachelor anyway. Turning away from the map, he headed into the kitchen to pour his second cup of coffee then returned to the map.

"Where should I go? What would be the perfect place to build my building."

Holding the cup to his lips for another sip, the cup covered a portion of the lower part of the map. Lowering the cup to see better, there it was in plain sight. The only State he had not visited. It was a State he first thought was too far from the current location of New York City. A Southern State steep in history and heritage. Everyone refers to this area as the 'Bible belt.' For that reason, he had initially kept it from consideration and for several other minor reasons.

It was the birthplace for the start of the civil war between the Northern aristocrats and the Southern good-old farm boys.

"What the heck," his mind said. It cannot hurt to investigate and since being, grounded from flying anywhere because of the weather through the weekend, I will take the time to study more on the State of South Carolina."

Off to the computer, Robert searched the internet for as much information as possible on the State of South Carolina. Robert discovered a plethora of information he had initially overlooked during his processing. This new discovery inspired more investigation.

Robert was now intrigued at the prospect of selecting a Southern State for his new venture.

The State had several reservoirs with rivers feeding into them for water activities. It harbored large acres of National and State forestry set aside in perpetuity. Several barrier islands for his employees to schedule vacations with family were a plus.

The old plantations that grew cotton and held slaves for labor were long gone; they were now more commercialized in the ways of growing crops. Most states had centers for the arts in every major city. Compatible with families to settle and want to stay.

The more Robert read online the more information he needed to know. His interest piqued.

A planned trip to the library to acquire written information related to South Carolina's history.

The Low Country

Spring was arriving in New York. It was time to get out of town. Robert divested himself in several forms of information found online, in libraries and bookstores about South Carolina. He was especially intrigued that the area was referred to as.

"The Low Country of South Carolina."

The next weekend he was ready, bags packed; the plane fueled, he completed preflight checks as quickly as possible. Robert now seated in his plane he throttled up the engine, racing down the runway he pulled the stick back to ascend to altitude for the trip to Charleston South Carolina.

The preselected Ford Bronco rental had been booked in advance of the trip. Robert headed to the Hertz car rental check-in point. Picking up the keys and finding the vehicle by pressing the lock button several times to listen for the horn. It was not parked in the spot his paperwork noted. "Must be a Southern thing down here," he thought.

Pulling up to the front of the Market Pavilion. The Valet took Roberts keys as the Doorman grabbed his luggage.

"Your luggage will be in your room right away Mr. Killings. Please see the clerk with the final check-in at the desk."

Robert pr-booked his stay as the attendant was ready for his prescribed arrival time.

"Here is your room key, Mr. Killings. You are on the concierge level near the elevator. There will be food available 24/7 with complimentary water or juice. Please help yourself."

The Market Pavilion Hotel is located on the corner of East Bay Street and South Market Street. It was specifically designed to resemble the architecture of an 18th century historic property. The Hotel displays some three hundred pieces of original art, including a George Washington portrait in the lobby bar.

Robert had prepared himself for exploration with many places on his list for consideration. Charleston was on his list along with a few upstate commercial areas and the low country of Beaufort, South Carolina, He decided to see this magnificent city and its waterfront restaurants.

First on his list was Charleston, South Carolina, and its rich diversity of history. Located in the marshy coastal plains, it became one of the richest and most powerful cities during the colonial era where the downtown street remains to this day set with cobblestones.

A major shipping port during those years for moving products up the coastline. Its location benefited from the surrounding plantations that grew indigo, cotton and rice with a plethora of seafood, oysters, fresh shrimp, and fish round out the delicacies this town has to offer.

The darker side of Charleston was the old slave trade. Where African people were, captured by the British, brought to the Americas and Charleston to be, displayed at a market for purchase or sold and forced to work on the southern plantations.

The old Market place is now a modern-day flea market for local farmers, artists, and craftsman to sell their wares.

Robert walked along the market, then to the area called the battery. Admiring the architecture, he stood and gazed at the creative craftmanship from the century's old buildings. Sculptured ornamental hand carved wood adorned the front of the buildings.

Fort Sumter was next on his list. The confederacy fired on the Fort on April 12, 1861, opening the civil war which redefined America.

Robert kept searching. Visiting South Carolina's barrier islands of Hilton Head, Edisto, and Fripp. Concluding the low country was not the place for his building. Although the workforce was sufficient, it was more of a retirement, vacation type community.

He further concluded he would be required to redesign his dream building to fit in with era specific history. Every detail he had sketched on his napkins and in his mind would have been a waste of time.

The search would continue for a more favorable location with common ground in the South for his design to be accepted.

Spartanburg / Greenville South Carolina. Aptly named the 'Upstate' area by the locals, had a large industrial presence. These cities were growing fast. Every type of business was being built. Checking only a few boxes on his spreadsheet. This area was overwhelmed with a steady need for professionals to staff the number of commercial and industrial complexes that were moving into the area. The competition for these corporations to find and keep employees was too much to consider relocating here. It received a big red X.

Robert saved the city he thought was going to be his redeeming feature for last on this trip of discovery.

Columbia, South Carolina, the state's Capital city is located about two hours South of Spartanburg / Greenville. Driving down interstate 26, Robert entered into another silent thinking process.

Robert again began envisioning the construction of his building. The moving of employees and the process of presenting all of this to the board of directors.

"This place has to work. I am running out of options."

Before he knew it, Robert had driven to the outskirts of Columbia, South Carolina. Not paying attention to his speed as he should. He noticed vehicles darting around him, honking horns, and yelling obscenities as they drove by.

Robert felt right at home. This place had just as many adversaries as his driving habits as his hometown of New York.

Finding the South Carolina State house on Gervais Street. He found a parking spot. Pulling a few quarters from his pocket to deposit into the meter. He was off on a walk around the city.

Robert immediately felt comfortable walking the streets of downtown Columbia. The people were kind and considerate. There was an abundance of helpful people when he found himself lost and had to ask for directions back to his vehicle. Although he respected and struggled to understand the Southern dialect, he knew it would be a challenge to learn.

Robert returned to his car one last time. He was full of excitement that this city was topping his list and checking all the boxes for his dream office building.

Reaching in his trousers to retrieve the cars key fob. He pressed the unlock button as two ladies were walking by. They were looking up at the sky, pointing and commenting on the vapor trail of an airplane some thirty thousand feet above them.

Robert turned to look up in the same direction they were pointing. There on the side of an old red brick building was a one-word sign embedded in the brick with faded paint.

'ADLUH'

It was the name of a grain milling company as old as Columbia itself. The original paint had stood the test of time and as many weather systems. The old company produced flour and cornmeal for centuries and shuttered long ago. Taking some time, he studied the building and its location. Robert concluded the building had been vacant for some time and in need of repairs. Knowing this location was unsuitable for his building he quickly assumed the local design review board and the historic preservation society would be all over him if he decided to tear it down to erect his dream.

Looking down from the brick façade, Robert could see a large, weathered sign as faded as was the name on the building. It was a real-estate company's listing sign. Erected on a large open lot next to the building.

Robert re-locked the car door and proceeded to cross the street to get a closer look and find out who the agent was.

Closing in on the sign he could make out a few numbers, while others were covered with dirt. He assumed the South Carolina weather had blown enough dust on it to obscure the numbers, the dusting provided layers of filth over the phone number.

Wiping away the debris, Robert copied the agent's name and number then headed back to the rental. It was beginning to sprinkle a light sultry shower. Enough to dampen the street and kick up the Southern humidity.

Robert grabbed a napkin from a fast-food bag and wiped the rain and sweat from his forehead. Reaching for his cell phone, he dials the number from the sign.

The phone begins to connect, Robert listens to a few rings before it is automatically answered via voicemail, He listens to a sweet southern voice of an older country lady as he struggles to understand her Southern accent. Opting out of leaving a message he ends the call to first ponder if he is doing the right thing. Now sitting in the rental, staring across the street at the sign, he picks up his phone to re-dial the number. To his surprise it was answered on the first ring.

"Good afternoon you have reached Mary Beth of Sherman and Hemstreet realtors. How can I help you?"

"Um Hello Mary, I am calling about..."

Mary Beth cuts off Robert before he can finish another word in his introduction.

"Honey, it is Mary Beth, Not Mary! My name is, Mary Beth."

"My apologies, Mary Beth. I am calling about a lot for sale on Gervais Street next to a building with the word ADLUH on the side of it. Can you give me some information on this listing?"

"Oh Sweetie, that lot has been for sale for about six to seven years. The old goat of a man that, owns it is pricing it too high. No one is willing to pay the premium price he set for it. I am the listing agent. Sometimes I feel it's a waste of my time putting sugar in that glass of tea, it isn't going to change the flavor, and his biscuits don't rise like the rest of us, if you know what I mean, honestly, I think he's missing some ingredients."

Before Robert can open his mouth to respond Mary Beth continues to talk. Keeping Robert at bay.

"Listen sugar, I am about to pick up my grandkids from karate class and they take priority over my real estate transactions, and I doubt you will want that piece of property when you hear the price. But darling I have more property I can show you. Let me call you back in a couple of hours when I get these little hellions out of my car and drop them off at their momma's and talk with my daughter for a bit then I will call you right back. Does that sound ok to you? I did not catch your name darling, what is it again?"

"I am Robert Killings Jr. Mary Beth."

"Alrighty sugar I will call you later."

Robert waited a few hours for Mary Beth to return his call. Continuing to drive around the city of Columbia before driving back to the airport in Charleston.

Two hours had passed, then three, then four. The sun was close to settling on the horizon when he decided it was time to retreat back to New York. Entering the coordinates into the navigation system. The CarPlay selected voice began delivering detailed instructions for the fastest route to his destination.

Robert was driving as he sat comfortably in the driver's seat listening to classic rock music from the eighties. As the music began to fade from his ears. His inner voice recalled his conversation with Mary Beth.

"She was right? That is not the perfect spot for the new office.

Robert's thoughts continued in his head.

"I have not received a call back or a text from Mary Beth. It is true what they say about these Southern people. Laid back, let us not get in a hurry, barely motivated, the ingrained mentality, I will get to it eventually. This woman would never make it as a real estate agent in New York."

Robert's mind was reset after hearing the annoying but alerting bell dinging in the vehicle. Music was still playing as the ding continued. 'Fuel Low' was his reminder from the dash, he needed to find a filling station within the next fifty miles.

The next exit off I 26 had fuel and food. Exiting from the interstate, Robert pulled into a station and began fueling the Ford Bronco Quickly grabbing a snack and a drink from inside the station, it was time to get back to driving the final leg of his journey.

Robert had driven some fifty additional miles before looking at his phone. The display shows a missed call with a voicemail from Mary Beth. She had tried calling while he was in the store away from his phone.

Robert did not like to use the phone while driving. The urge to listen to what Mary Beth had to say was too great, he decided he could at least listen to the voicemail.

Watching his driving, Robert carefully set the phone on the passenger seat while skillfully starting the voicemail option. Mary Beth's sweet southern voice filled the vehicle.

"Hey there Mr. Robert Killings Jr. I am so sorry I took all this time before calling you back. You see honey, my daughter needed to talk. So, we left the kids with her husband while her and I, well we went and had us a couple big margaritas at Theresa's Mexican restaurant. Then some of my girlfriends joined us. I can confess we had us a good old girl scout meeting."

"I am calling you back with some information on that property. If you might still be interested. You know I would not be doing my job if I did not call you back. Now Suga try not to be mad at me, but I was having an enjoyable time with them, Margaritas. Well, listen honey, it might be better if you call me tomorrow because I am too tipsy right now to talk anyway. So, let us not put too much butter in them grits tonight. I need to go to bed. Call me tomorrow SUGA!"

Robert could not believe what he had just listened to. To grasp the full scope of the conversation he replayed the voicemail three times. Not used to listening to a woman such as Mary Beth's Southern drawl. Her accent was like no other he had ever experienced before now.

Robert quickly recalled he was South of the Mason Dixon line. An imaginary boundary that characterizes a cultural and linguistic difference from his Northern roots. This Southern language was, developed over a course of several hundred years from plantation life and the influx of immigrants from many cultures meshing into one style of language.

He deliberated with himself.

"Could this move to the South work out?"

Only time will tell, he assumed. If and when his time would come to run the company. He had to be ready with a decision. Choosing the right place was a serious decision. He knew he could succeed if given the chance. He studied his Fathers business profile and felt he was ready if he were to assume the business from his Father.

If he did nothing to prepare ahead of time, he would always feel the board and his clients may never give him the respect he deserved if he chooses to stay in the big Apple. It was a major move and the best for everyone to start controlling the corporation with a new perspective in a new city with his direction.

It was the dawn of a new day. Robert could not sleep well in his suite at the Market Pavilion. Checking out and tipping the bell hop as keys to the rental were returned to him. The short drive to the airport was a somber tone. No radio, no thinking.

Arriving at the airport, Robert returned the rental and began the task of loading his luggage onto his plane. Buckling himself into the pilot's chair while contemplating his thoughts.

"When should I call Mary Beth?"

She was not in a hurry to return his call in a timely manner. Opting to go drinking with the girls and her daughter took precedents over a real estate transaction. Robert decided to let her wait until he was back home.

Robert finished his preflight checklist and began to taxi the plane to the runway; It was time to fly this bird back to New York.

The Southern Charm of Mary Beth

Robert settled back into his comfortable apartment in New York city. The trip to South Carolina filled his thoughts daily. A few more calls to Mary Beth were in order.

Dialing Mary Beth was not easy for Robert. She had an impressive way with words. With her high-pitched voice, she sounded like a carnival princes instead of a realtor. Some words he understood plainly, and others were a mix of sound waves that came out too fast as one long octave of sound preventing his ability to grasp the meaning of while engaged in a conversation with her.

Mary Beth was a true southern lady, born and raised in the South. She was full of life while embracing the meaning of it. A Southern Babtist, raised to attend church every Sunday. She volunteered for every event the church scheduled. Baking pies, cakes, or cookies for all the functions. Mary Beth loved singing in the choir. Although she could not carry a tune. She found it encouraging to give it her best.

One Wednesday afternoon at practice, the other girls in the choir took Mary Beth off the stage for a stern southern, "Bless your heart" a sort of 'woman to woman,' let us get something straight here girl conversation.

Mary Beth took the advice and began stepping to the back of the choir so she would not be noticed. The hymns were sung in silence, only her lips were moving without sound.

She was a professional player at any game. Real estate was her best choice for success. Putting her musical career on hold.

Mary Beth was leaving another listing appointment when her phone began to ring. It was Robert calling again.

Staring at the phone with a smug Southern look on her face. She knew where this conversation was headed before she would answer. Quickly changing into her best attitude for Robert's call. She held the phone in her right hand as her large purse dangled by the straps across her same forearm. Pulling down her shades with her left hand she began her Southern stride to her awaiting vehicle. Touching the smart phone's green button, her delightful Southern charm kicked in.

"Why hello Mr. Killings, So, good to hear from you, honey."

Before Robert could begin his conversation, Mary Beth took control of the call again with everything she had.

"Now look here suga, I know why you are calling. I have been in contact with Mr. Richardson. Let me see, It was yesterday I believe. If not, yesterday was the day before. I can check my calendar to verify that if you need me too. I realize you want to make an offer on that parcel. But in all honesty sweetie he is an old bagger set in his ways.

Now, Robert, I have conveyed all this to you once already and I am not being miss snippy pants, You should listen to the advice I will give you concerning this property. I have years of experience in this part of the country. The old goat of a man is sitting tight on his pricing, and it will take an act of congress or a bolt of lightning to make him sell it at an offer below his asking price. Listen to me darling, I am a smart lady, and I deserve some respect."

Silence was Robert's response. He had grown impatient listening to Mary Beth ramble for the time being and drifted off into one of his own thoughts again. Unaware Mary Beth was still talking.

Mary Beth took a short breather from her speech. There was no response from Robert, thinking he might have hung up on her she decided to yell on the phone.

"HELLO, Mr. Killings, are you there? "Gosh dang it, did you hang up on me?"

The increased volume from Mary Beth startled Robert back to reality.

"Yes, Mary Beth I am still here listening to you although I did relapse in my own thoughts. So, I missed a good bit of your speech."

"I apologize, Mr. Killings. I sometimes get carried away."

"Mary Beth, I will be coming down to South Carolina again soon. I will email you my proposal to submit to Mr. Richardson. Please look it over before I arrive."

"May I ask what it is you plan to offer before you; email me something I may consider the offer a waste of time? I have conveyed the circumstances. He will not budge on his price. Mr. Richardson thinks that property has oil or gold under it."

"As you are aware Mary Beth, like Mr. Richardson, I am in no hurry to purchase the property anytime soon. I do in fact want to secure the parcel so no one else will be able to purchase the property without me getting first rights of refusal."

"So, with that said. I plan to give him an offer to lease the land to me at its current value. With a contingency to finalize our arrangement with first rights of refusal if he gets an offer to purchase the property at his full asking price. This should seal a deal with him and get the property off the market until I have control of Killings insurance LLC."

"Well, I will be a monkey's uncle. Mr. Killings, you are smarter than a possum crossing the road in daylight. This just might get that old stallion to the water trough after all. Send that email and I will write the offer as soon as I can get back into the office tomorrow. Right now, it is margarita time with the girls. Bye suga."

"Goodbye Mary Beth."

Roberts plan for the future was coming together. Putting the pieces together now was his modus operandi. It did not make sense to wait for the inevitable to start the process. He was a patient man mixed with intelligent due diligence.

"Patience defines a man with a plan."

Robert ascertained he was better off waiting to send the email until Monday as it was already getting late on

Friday. His conversation with Mary Beth had given him caution in his thinking she was going to be into the margaritas soon and sending the proposal now would spell disaster if she tried to call Mr. Richardson to explain the details of the proposed contract while self-medicated.

He didn't mention to Mary Beth that he wanted to join her meeting with Mr. Richardson.

Robert was becoming concerned that this Queen of the South may not be presenting the proposal in good faith. Given the fact she knows this man all too well, something just did not add up properly. He pondered his request to be present with Mary Beth when his offer was submitted may not be kosher within her real estate world. He did not care at this point. No more games from Mary Beth.

Robert began the preparations for another return flight to Columbia, South Carolina.

Robert always called his mother to let her know his plans when he decided to fly out of town. She worried about her only son flying solo. Providing her with details of his flight schedule seemed to give her comfort and he was happy to oblige her requests regarding his flight information.

Robert kept his plans a secret. No one, neither his mother nor his father was unaware of the original plan he was about to embark on.

It was how he wished it to be. Letting people in on a secret could become an explosive disaster. Gossip can ruin the best creative enterprise. Details begin to emerge as speculation can become a reality in someone's eyes. A leak to the wrong news media and the whole thing gets torn apart as they attempt to analyze your next move and report on speculation.

Employees can jump ships to competitors. Stock in the company can crash in an instant. Rumors can become hurtful to a company's portfolio. Customers cancel policies with concerns the company is failing. There are many reasons Robert needed to retain secrecy of every detail of his plan.

Robert surmised one day his father would retire or he would acquire it under duress of circumstance out of his control.

Robert landed in Columbia, South Carolina early that Saturday morning. Once set in his hotel he began searching the internet for Architects worthy of helping design and managing the construction of the building he had in mind.

He knew there would be some modifications to his design he had to consider for one simple reason. It was the South. Not New York. This city had culture and lots of history to contend with. Hiring an architectural consultant for the area of construction was first on his list. Gathering a list of companies to contact if and when Mr. Richardson agreed to his terms. The words of Mary Beth came to mind. He needed to get this old stallion to the water trough.

Evening had come early for Robert. Once dinner was finished at a local eatery he retired from his hotel, got a shower then laid in bed and fell asleep.

Forgetting to close the hotel window shades, Robert awakened to the Sunday sunshine beaming through the window. Heading downstairs to look for a coffee shop. First stop at the receptions desk to ask for directions to a coffee shop close enough for a short walk. The gentleman behind the counter took a moment to look Robert over as he replied.

"Sir, this is Columbia, South Carolina. The heart of the Bible belt. Nothing opens on Sunday until after church."

Robert could not believe what he had just heard. "This cannot be true. Everything is open in New York, all night every night."

He had to experience this phenomenon himself. Stepping out onto the parking lot he understood the gravity of the situation. Very few people were stirring about the downtown area. In New York, these streets would be moving like ants on an anthill.

Robert stood still as he breathed in the crisp morning air. What am I listening to? The local bells from a nearby church were ringing. The sound resonated off the surrounding buildings. It was a calling he could not ignore. He needed to know more about this so-called Bible belt Robert rushed back to his room. Opening the door with his electronic key, he stepped to the nightstand next to his bed. There in the drawer he found a small Bible.

Clutching it in his hand, Robert headed out the front glass doors of the Hotel to find the source of the bells.

Walking briskly, he searched for the source of the beautiful sound he was drawing too. The bells had fallen silent. Robert was standing at the foot of a set of granite steps leading up to a set of large double doors that were now closed. As he stood by himself, he could hear singing from inside the church. Slowly he advanced up the steps to the grand doorway. Grasping the gold handle, Robert gave it a pull.

Inside the church doors were two Black men. Assuming they were the ushers. One turned to Robert to greet him.

"Welcome my brother. I can assist you in finding a seat in one of the church pews if you would like to follow me."

Entering a second set of doors past the main entrance, Robert was ushered to an empty seat about halfway through the congregation.

His eyes were wide open as he realized he had entered an all-Black church where everyone was engaged in singing and dancing. The choir was leading the chorus with clapping and praises.

Then silence as the reverend approached the front of the stage.

He quickly picked out Robert as a new guest.

"I see we have a visitor amongst us."

At that point, all eyes were trained on Robert.

"In this house everyone is welcome. Could you please stand and tell us who you are my good man?"

Robert stood as the stares continued. At that moment he understood the meaning of the cliché'

"I am the cream in the Oreo cookie."

"I am Robert Killings jr. sir. If it pleases you, I would like to attend your services today."

"All are welcome in this house my son. Let us all welcome Mr. Killings."

At that moment, every person attending service called out at the same moment.

"Welcome Mr. Killings."

Monday arrives and Robert calls Mary Beth.

"Hello Mary Beth. I decided I will accompany you today to deliver the proposal to Mr. Richardson. I do understand this is an unprecedented procedure, but I need to be present to answer any questions he might have. It is time I took control of the negotiating with Mr. Richardson on a face-to-face basis. No disrespect but nothing else has worked for you in the past attempt to secure a sale on that parcel."

"Look here honey, I take my job seriously and I work for you. There is no fox in 'this' hen house mister if that is what you are implying."

"Listen closely Mary Beth. You and I both need to have this meeting today with Mr. Richardson or I will pull the deal. I will find another location; You lose your commission. The city of Columbia, South Carolina loses a half billion dollars of investment into the local economy.

It will be on you to explain to the local Mayor, and your state representatives will not appreciate your failure to secure a sweetheart deal once they find out you alone botched it. Your reputation as a realtor will be finished in this town. I would not be surprised if they did not run you out of town."

Robert hesitated, waiting for her response when Mary Beth finally comments.

"Since you so graciously pointed out the wonderful advantages of your investment in our community along with addressing the consequences we face here. I am sure I can bend the rules a tiny bit, just for you Mr. Killings, JUNIOR!"

"Thank you for accepting my offer to help negotiate on our behalf, Mary BETH! Now pick me up when Mr. Richardson agrees to the time to discuss the proposal. I will be waiting for your call."

"Yessir, I am on it like a June bug on a…."

"Do not say it Mary Beth, just do not say it. Goodbye."

"I usually leave a conversation with a nice southern goodbye with a "see you soon suga," But I think you need to change the oil in your tractor if you plan to move your company down South."

A brief time later in the day, Robert received a text from Mary Beth's phone. {2:00 PM} was all that was on the phone's screen as Robert assumed she was still a little put out of their earlier conversation.

Mary Beth pulled into the hotel's drop-off area. Unlocked the door for Robert. Once inside and buckled up she gave the car some gas and sped away to Mr. Richardsons office as she remained silent until they arrive. Once parked, Mary Beth spoke to Robert.

"Before you get out and get all high and mighty, I need to let you know Mr. Richardson is my cousin. We have not had the best relationship, so if we have words between us, in front of you. You will just have to get over it."

Robert decided it was better at that moment to keep his thoughts to himself. The voice in his head was rolling with the news Mary Beth decided to declare with him before the meeting would begin.

Robert had a sixth sense about people that gained him notoriety in the industry. He keyed in on body language and word salads people used while overseeing arbitrating settlements for several claims over the years. He was a keen negotiator when it came to contract closures.

Robert knew there was something between these two that was holding up previous deals with this property and the cards Mary Beth just laid out on the table changed the game in his favor.

Entering the office building, Robert was not surprised at all when the front desk receptionist stood up to embrace his agent.

"Mary Beth, so, happy to see you again. How are your daughters? Those grand babies must be getting on up there."

Robert heard what he needed to hear in that greeting. Mary Beth had not entered this building in a while. Much less talk to her cousin face to face for the same amount of time.

"Is the old goat in the office?" she asked the young slender receptionist.

"Why yes ma'am, he sure is. I will let him know you are here for a visit. Can I let him know what this is about?" asked the receptionist.

"Yes, of course you may. I have a client with me. A Mr. Killings jr. He is interested in the lot cousin Charles is selling."

"Oh goody, He wants to get rid of that parcel as soon as he can."

Mary Beth was obviously becoming unsettled with that proclamation from the young woman. She never once looked at Robert. Just began fiddling with her purse and adorning jewelry she had on.

Robert cringed slightly at receiving this information. Thinking to himself,

"This gets deeper every minute I am here."

Professional businesspeople process information quickly. A sound decision based on information can make or break a deal. Robert began deliberating the thought of walking away at this moment. It was indeed a challenging decision he needed to make. Although staying on the course will prove to be rewarding if he can seal this deal today. First, he needed an answer to a critical issue.

"Why did Mary Beth decide not to convey his offers to her cousin, Mr. Charles Richardson?"

Following close behind Mary Beth, the two enter the office to find an older man, Mr. Richardson sitting behind a desk piled with paperwork. The lines on his face told a story of challenging work or a life of drinking. Witnessing the man steadily typing on an ancient keyboard with each key weathered from aged greasy fingers as Charlie stared at an old CRT monitor proofing a manuscript he was typing out.

Robert gazed around the room as Charlie failed to acknowledge his or Mary Beths presence. While Mary Beth stood silent in front of Charlie, the man she referred to as the "old goat." Holding her purse with both hands, low and in front of her. Mary Beth began twisting back and forth from the hips. A classic motion when someone is about to get scolded.

Robert took this moment to assess the room. Dimly lit with well dated lamps. The curtain fabric hiding in the windows had a musk smell of old cigar smoke from days when it was acceptable to light one inside of a building. The two chairs in front of the desk were additional space for Chalie's paperwork. Unusable for sitting down and obvious to Robert, no one had tried in quite some time.

Charlie finished with one finger pecking away at the dirty keyboard, looking up to see Mary Beth standing nervously in front of him. Charlie leaned back in his office chair, as it creaked an odd noise of begging for oil while folding his hands together, placing them in his lap. With a solum voice he asked.

“What do you want Mary Beth?

Charlie had failed to notice Robert standing off to the side of the desk. Before she could respond, Robert leaned over the desk, extended his hand to Charlie, introducing himself.

Greeting Roberts’ handshake. Charlie’s eyes were still trained on Mary Beth as he repeated.

“I asked you a question little lady. Cat got your tongue?”

Mary Beths head hung low to her chest, never looking up at her cousin, he lite female voice replied.

“I brought Mr. Killings in to meet with you in person about the lot you are trying to sell.”

"Trying, you said TRYING! You are the one who is supposed to be trying. Why the H……"

Robert immediately intervened, avoiding a confrontation between the two cousins.

"Mr. Richardson. Please sir. I would like to discuss purchasing the land you have listed with Mary Beth. I have a decent offer for you to consider."

"Alright then, let us discuss this like gentlemen without Mary Beth in the room. You can leave now and do not let that door hit you in the ass on the way out."

Mary Beth turned to leave. As she pulled the door handle to open the old wooden door, she could not help but turn her head to have the last word with Charlie.

"You better not try to cut me out of my commission, you old goat, I earned this one."

Charlie stood up, walked around to the front of the desk to remove the pile of paperwork from one of his chairs. Dusted off the arm rest as he offered Robert the comfort of sitting for the negotiating process.

Robert wasted no time in conveying his offer to Charlie. The details of negotiating came easy to him. He had a mannerism about him people seemed comfortable with.

An abbreviated time later. The two men stood at the office door as they interrupted the old and young cackling hens waiting outside for them to emerge.

"Mary Beth, Lets go, said Robert. I will fill you in on the details of the proposal on the way back to my hotel. If you can write it up quickly enough, I can sign off on it before I fly back to New York."

Robert had secured the next chapter of his life.

The Passing

Robert was again off on one of his fact-finding adventures. While sitting down to dinner at a hometown restaurant, his cell phone began to disturb his thoughts with relentless vibrating.

Dismissing it as a cold call or scammer, he decides to finish his dinner and head to the hotel for the night. Besides, if it were important the caller would ring him again.

Minutes later the annoying vibration begins as he again dismisses the obnoxious device. The third time was a sequence needing attention. Deciding to let his steak sit idle he retrieves the sophisticated alerting device he had a vial distaste for.

Phones were meant for communication, when necessary. While at work, not when he was away on a trip. Everyone now advised never to call when he is away.

Deciding to look at checking the caller I.D.

It was a call from Mother. A quick thought entered his head, "Ignoring her would not go well." Selecting the green button on the glass face Robert answered.

"Hello Mother"

Mother was crying. Robert could barely make out her incoherent words as she struggled to communicate into the phone.

"It is about your father Robert. You need to come to my home, COME HOME NOW! Your dad has passed away, apparently, he suffered a massive heart attack at work. The paramedics did everything they could to save him."

Frantically she replied,

"I don't know what to do."

"Please try to calm down Mother. I will leave here as soon as I can."

Within an hour Robert's plane was airborne heading home.

The Death of Roberts father shocked the insurance industry. His father was an iconic figure in the local community, a man with a strong faith, which attended church regularly. His company supported local little league baseball teams and contributed heavily to charitable organizations often.

Everything in life can change instantly. It is our typical western culture of not being prepared for the passing of a loved one or ourselves. Too much emphasis is dedicated to material things we value more than preparing for the inevitable. Eastern cultures prepare for the end of life. Knowing it is a necessity to prepare for this transition.

Robert was prepared for this day. It was in his DNA. He immediately took the initiative and began the task of planning the funeral.

Other necessities were required as well. Such as a caterer capable of providing food for large crowds at the celebration of life.

Robert's father had amassed many friends during his life span of eighty years. Notifying everyone personally was an enormous challenge. Robert was astonished at the multitude of professional entrepreneurs, acquaintances, friends, or friends. His Father knew everyone. The people he knew comprised of everyone in New York. Robert's mother agreed to hold the celebration of life at their residence on Staten Island. The residence held fond memories of birthdays and celebrations on the beach with friends. His father had asked his mom for her hand in marriage on the very spot where the house was built.

Robert's father had wished for cremation. The thought of laying horizontal in a coffin in eternity churned his stomach just thinking about it.

Robert knew it was his responsibility to greet local friends and dignitaries from across the globe as they entered the doorway to his parents' home, shaking hands, accepting hugs and condolences from everyone. Being the only child and his father's son, it was his right of passage to receive each guest. Throughout the night Robert became overwhelmed with countless personal stories conveyed about his father.

It was now time to say goodbye to friends and business associates, as the last group departed the house, Robert closed the front door behind the last person. Pausing to collect himself, he slowly turned away from the door. There standing behind him was his mother. She was herself very calm. He knew he had her genes as well as his father's. He could tell there was something on her mind.

"Robert, can we chat for a moment before you leave? Come sit on the veranda with me, I need a bourbon and pour yourself a scotch, no need to waste any time on matters needing attention today."

With a fresh rocks glass full of bourbon in hand, she takes a sip.

Mother begins.

"I know you are fully away I have been a devoted stay-at-home spouse to your father. Never have I indulged in the business affairs. It was his request for me to be a well-kept homemaker, ready to entertain guests at any moment. Your father always needed to secure an important personnel meeting to discuss business.

We have kept a close watch on the progress of your career. You have built for yourself one of the best. Your Father and I are enormously proud of you.

I want you to understand one thing. The business is yours to manage fittingly if I am to be kept in this house and my affairs taken care of by the company as they were when your father was alive."

"Without question, Mother, I assure you everything will remain the same. I will see to it myself, just as my father would see it. With that said, Mother, I feel it necessary to convey to you my long-term plan of moving the company to Columbia South Carolina. I would like your blessing of course."

Robert spent the next three hours with his mother explaining his plan, his dream, how it came about in great detail. Cheryl Killings sat in silence while Robert filled her ears with seamless detail after detail.

Finaly Robert's voice fell silent, beginning to contemplate his mother's response. His babbling must be boring to her, she has said nothing.

"Robert, my son. You are a genius." I support you in full. We shall schedule a board meeting immediately announcing the start of a new tenure for you as CEO of Killings insurance LLC. It was your father's wishes as described in detail in his last will and testament."

Letters were sent to the board of directors with instructions to gather collectively in the boardroom of Killings Insurance LLC as quickly as possible to vote on the urgent order of business presented to them.

The members were all present as each of their names, read aloud in a roll call procession.

The order of business is as prescribed. We, the board of directors, hereby nominate Robert Killings Jr. as directed in our bylaws by vote of confidence to confirm as the new CEO of Killings insurance, LLC.

Every board member and top employees had a chance to voice their approval of Robert before each ballot was tallied.

Robert Killings Jr. is now unanimously elected as the CEO, a moment marked by smiles and handshakes that filled the room. He wasted no time sharing his ambitious vision for the company's future. His plan was to relocate to a new state. A Southern State, complete with a brand-new building.

Reaching into his wallet, he pulled out a napkin. With a sense of pride, he held it aloft.

"This," he declared, "is our dream. This is our future."

His words echoed in the room, leaving a profound impact as the room erupted into applause. Everyone rose to their feet, their claps resonating with enthusiasm. Shouts.

"Woo-hoo! We are with you, Robert," filled the air, a testament to their unwavering support.

Robert felt a sense of accomplishment. His strong work ethics had earned him the respect of everyone present. Now, it was his time to turn his dream into reality. It was time to implement the plan.

With the meeting adjourned Robert felt the need to visit every board member to personally thank them for their support as his father would have done the same. He sat with each executive individually to outline his plan in greater detail. Robert believed each person involved with the company should have full transparency in understanding the outcome of each phase of the plan. This should include information on selecting architects' construction engineers and downstream contractors erecting the building. His choice to use unionized labor drew acceptance from the board members.

Robert left the board meeting and headed home. His pride was at an all-time high. The board overwhelmingly approved of his plan for the future of the corporation.

He began to slip into his thoughts as he walked to his apartment. Each footstep began to silently whisper away. The physical movement of walking was now an unknown action. He pondered.

"Would his father approve of this?"

He had never found the time to discuss it with him. The sadness of losing his father came to the forefront of his thoughts. He walked in silence as a tear formed on his cheek. Still looking up at the buildings and the lack of architecture, a part of his daily routine.

"What would the old man think of me now?"

All those flights to city after city. Analyzing the details of each location, keeping the plan to himself. The pros and cons are meticulously written on a spread sheet. Day after

Day and Month after Month. Flying back and forth gathering as much information as he could.

The decision had come down to one city he admired the most.

The company was moving to Columbia, South Carolina

The Concept

Robert met with the Architectural design team once a week to discuss each detail of the buildings design. Sharing his thoughts of approval or disapproval during the initial drawing phase. The layout of where each department and the workflow. Nothing was left out of the plans. He had every detail worked out, right down to where the restrooms would be located for ease of access.

It was a process to ensure the final placement of work-space need not ever require renovations or improvements for years to come.

Robert would continue to adjust wall locations and cubical space daily, bringing a piece of paper or a napkin to the architect's office for review and implementation into the final drawings. Several months had passed with multiple visits and meetings to hand out his ideas.

The architect had enough and stopped Robert at the door to his office, preventing Robert from entering. He needed to halt the constant changes to the drawings which were delaying the start of the project's bidding phase. The lead architect looked at Robert and said,

"These concept drawings are complete, it will take nearly two years to complete construction or longer with the present design, if we continue to address every change or idea you come up with, this building will never get built, much less select a date to start construction."

Robert stood fast and nodded in agreement,

"Ok, I can live with that."

Once and only once did Robert second guess his plan would not pass the approval of the board. But they all knew, if the company was to survive and grow, the concept must have approval soon.

Another meeting of the board members and executives of satellite branches convened the next week. Robert's design team of architects and engineers were present to field the curious questioning. Robert thought the four-hour parley of questions would never end. Robert stood at the end of the solid oak conference table his dad commissioned from a woodworking specialist in Washington state. A long oval shaped table made of thick western black oak with dark epoxy winding back and forth from one end to the other. His dad called it a river table. The topcoat was a clear epoxy, so clearly it reflected the overhead lighting from it. Robert now consumed by his father's words he could hear from inside his mind. It was as if his dad spoke to him in person, again explaining the table at which he was now staring down at.

Robert snapping back from the inner trance, noticing he clearly was now the center of attention as all eyes were on him.

With a sharp executive voice, Robert asked the assembly of executive one final question.

"Are we unanimous in our decision to accept these plans as drawn and move forward? "

"All ye in favor say you now, I?"

Robert felt joy in the room. Not a single descent to his question.

Erecting forty stories of concrete, steel, and glass, complete with a secure underground car park. The façade's design was as a brilliant structure with an appealing look of acceptance. A building concept with a grandeur 19th century style Porte'-cochere normally used in European design or a modern-day reproduction used for the entrance to a fancy Las Vegas casino.

It took two years to complete. Robert Killings reasoning was a simple one. Take Killings insurance LLC to the next level. The plan was to initially occupy the upper ten floors for day-to-day operations. This will adequately provide the space needed, giving the company four additional floors than the existing overcrowded workspace here in New York. Another ten floors below will be set aside for future expansion.

The remaining lower floors were set aside for commercial retail space. This move would generate rental income that would recoup some, if not all the construction costs in the years to come.

The one exception to this beautiful structure was his personal penthouse which of course would encompass the entire footprint of the top floor of the building. Robert assessed the safety of residing where he worked and would grant quick access to decisions for the company.

The thought of navigating traffic or even walking to work was not in the scheme of life anymore. Living in New York will change you. Another creative idea all in its own. Robert deliberated for hours on end with the penthouse design. It was the last section of the building he needed to finish creating. This would be his home and sanctuary away from the long hours of business pressures with the comfort of having guests for cocktails and dinner.

Robert had gathered ideas for the penthouse collectively from the many establishments he visited in his worldly travels as a single man. The living room was a spacious room with exterior glass walls allowing for a spectacular view while sitting on his antique furniture purchased years ago, stored in a climate-controlled space for the day to come he would have his home built. Only one bedroom is needed. There were no initial plans for a family, but they envisioned Mrs. Killings someday. Off the bedroom he added two walk-inn closets big enough to sleep in if he was ever kicked out of bed. The Architect jokingly asked if he planned to store a Volkswagen in one.

Robert killings jr. was a brilliant man that stood tall and proud. He shook hands with a strong grip. Everyone felt the strength that commanded respect as a confident CEO. He treated each and all the same, without regard to who you were or your stature in life. Robert was a scholar with an MBA, from Columbia university in New York.

A seasoned aviator. He loved flying the corporate jet. Shying away from the newer experimental planes his fellow aviators enjoyed. They were all too risky to fly as he could not entertain the thought of someone else taking his company and selling off assets if he perished in one of those garage-built makeshift paper planes as he often referred to them.

Once revered to as a visionary genius that could imagine a project from start to finish. This new office structure was no different. Years would pass with many a napkin stored away for future reference before the building final concept would become an electronic C.A.D drawing for presentation and acceptance by the company's executive board.

To keep up with years of thought, he decided to begin scribbling his dream on a lone piece of bar napkin, he could visualize the finished building standing alone as a pinnacle to the community. It was always in the dream in his head.

The time had come to move the corporate office and transition into an office larger than the overcrowded building in downtown bustling high-rise in downtown New York. The process of selecting the right demographics for the company was long overdue. The move to the more serene setting of Columbia, South Carolina selected out of ten other cities.

The challenges of moving a large fortune five-hundred company were enormous. A real estate company specializing in relocation processing now selected. High ranking officers and executive personnel residence were listed on the MLS. Some homes required the real estate agency to purchase homes of select employees allowing them to proceed with contracting with an agent for a new one in South Carolina.

Only the top one hundred employees were provided with relocation assistance from the corporation. While some chose retirement and others found similar roles elsewhere, two hundred decided to part ways with the company. The relocation package provided substantial support for those making significant moves across several states. Robert, fully aware, his employees were to be relocated away from their familiar surroundings. Despite the two-year preparation period, the decision was not easy for many, as they had to consider family, children's education, and friendships before making the final decision.

Once the relocations were completed, the company faced the task of filling the vacancies. One solution was to hire local talent through temporary staffing agencies. These new hires would initially be on a temporary contract, with a one-year evaluation period before transitioning to permanent employment.

Robert, the head of Killings Insurance LLC, took pride in personally addressing everyone in the company. His caring nature made him a beloved leader, but he was not one to be, taken lightly. Making it clear to all who met him, he preferred to be, addressed simply as "Robert," a testament to his approachable and down-to-earth leadership style.

Fifteen years prior to his father's passing and assuming helm as CEO to managing the corporation. He was just an employee at another mega insurance firm.

Until he succeeded his father, the ideas and ambitions would have to stay folded away in his wallet. Although patience was a virtue he possessed.

He once concluded that, ignoring the desire to slow down and think through a high-risk decision such as this one is how most "would be" entrepreneurs fail miserably. Failure carries a high degree of consequences for everyone involved.

The plan, the concept, will someday become reality. It was not his turn yet. First, he would build the trust all great men had come accustomed to acquiring.

His father provided wisdom and encouragement with kind direction as he grew up. He could never forget one such declaration.

"Destiny fills our souls, you either lead, follow or get out of the way. Two percent of the population run the world, three percent follow the two percent diligently, the rest just get out of the way."

Robert overslept the next morning. Grabbing a quick coffee at the local corner stand he headed out of town to the airport. Fueled up the Cessna for a long flight down to Columbia, South Carolina. Robert needed to meet with the bankers to fund the construction project. The paperwork was ready to sign. Once signed the initial funds were to be transferred to a separate account. He would then notify the Architects and Engineers to begin the first phase of letting the project out for bid. Robert Killings Jr. had just taken the first step towards a future he had only dreamed about for fifty plus years.

That Napkin

The sun was setting on the western skyline of the city; it was of course New Yorks West side.

As the cool air began to dip between the skyscrapers. The walk to the club gave him comfort that his standard business suit would provide needed warmth when he decided to walk home.

It was Roberts' weekly routine of heading to the club, to begin the process of recalling his dream once again from memory to improve its design or just scribble random thoughts on a napkin while enjoying his favorite scotch.

Walking amongst the tall buildings, he critiqued the architect's vision. Each one employed a unique signature, specific to the firm commissioned to construct these behemoth buildings. Robert loathed seeing unappealing square boxes jutting up from the city streets, one after the other, they were all the same, void of any inspiration.

It was the end of September and winter was approaching. An enjoyable time to have his favorite Dewars, which he preferred neat. Sitting at the bar alone as usual, Rpbert glances at the interior ornate craftmanship. Built in the

1800's by carpenters with real trade skills from an era long ago.

A grand building that would stand alone as a pinnacle of architectural achievement. A creative idea so brilliant would win awards for its design.

Your usual Robert? asked the bartender.

"Yes, and thanks for referring to me as Robert."

"That is proper sir, I will get you your Dewars."

Robert preferred "Robert" versus Mr. Killings, a formal reference his father preferred.

The less formal version was more acceptable, lending a more pleasurable engagement upon meeting someone for the first time or long-term friendships. It would be his way of gaining status. It was easier to respect a man you considered an equal.

Robert recalled everyone called his father Mr. Killings. It was too authoritarian to him. Even the condensed version of Bob just never sounded good spoken to him.

Robert was single, not for any reason, marriage just never came about. College studies, business first, took precedence to dating on a serious level and children would hamper the long-term ambitions of success.

"Here is your Dewars Robert."

"You're a fine bartender, Nate, now make sure it's filled when it gets low, I may need the extra antifreeze as I walk home later."

"Absolutely, I will see to that and here are the extra napkins and a pen you always request."

Robert smiles as he thanks Nate for knowing his routine so well.

The process begins with a few sips of scotch, His memory of the building quickly recalled as all the activities surrounding him becomes less important. Hoisting the pen from the solid oak bar top. Robert begins the process of penning what would eventually become his life's crown jewel of achievement.

Scribbling once again, the ink transfers his thoughts to the napkin. Halfway through the process a second Dewars is, delivered. Robert's keen sense of smell reaches his nose, a subtle, sweet perfume from a woman.

The drawing on the napkin engulfed his thoughts so profoundly he had failed to notice someone had been sitting next to him until an aroma aroused his curiosity. Breaking away from his normal unwavering concentration. A protocol of solitude suited him better than interacting in groups or single members with small meaningless intoxicated small talk of daily business or stock market investments. He chose to concentrate on his dream and the napkin.

"A single moment in time, your curiosity or the scent of a woman's perfume can change your life forever."

Roberts acute sense of smell was getting the best of him. Setting his pen down was not something he normally does until he is ready to cash out and go home. His future was on that napkin.

Reaching for the refilled glass of scotch immersed around a big square ice cube. The bigger the ice cube the larger the sound it made clinking against its captive container.

Raising the scotch, he stopped short of his lips. To his right, a mere half an arm's length sat the source of the sweet subtle fragrance. No man has a crystal ball. No man knows what the future will hold for him. No man controls his destiny like Robert Killings, jr.

Stheno is a gorgon in Greek mythology. She has two sisters. She and her sister Euryale were immortal, and the

third sister Medusa was mortal. Medusa is the Queen who turns people into stones with her eyes.

Dewars in hand inches from Robert's lips, he felt like a stone statue, unable to move or speak. Stunned beyond imagination. Frozen in time, his eyes struggle to focus inside the club's dim lighting.

His thoughts were racing. Realizing his fingers are going numb while holding the cold cocktail glass. Robert's eyes began to water as if he had not blinked for several seconds. Realizing she was staring at the napkin with the same intensity of concentration while he scribbled. He begins thinking.

"She must've been watching me the entire time I have been doodling on this napkin."

He is still frozen like the cliché' (Deer in the headlights) as if time had stopped just for this moment. He can hear the voice in his head ask all the questions. Who? who is this beautiful woman sitting next to him, when did she sit down? Where did she come from? Robert stepped out of his comfort zone, ignoring everyone.

Robert could not believe what he was experiencing as she lifted her head, ever so slowly, turning to look directly into Robert's eyes.

His mind again starts reacting with thoughts as if he were in a dream.

"That hair, what beautiful green eyes."

Ever so slowly her lips change from the intensity of deep thoughts to an embracing smile.

She begins a conversation.

"Interesting drawing. Are you in engineering or a design Architect?"

Robert stunned at her voice, staring at her face, unable to respond, no emotion. All he could muster was a poker face, there is a dead silence in the club as his hearing had momentarily shut down. His mind is blank, unable to utter a response to her question.

Am I in a movie? His mind asks.

Robert snaps back to reality with her next question.

"Hello! anybody in there?"

Just before she takes a sip of wine.

Now out of his trance, YES! Yes, of course, I mean No, I am not an architect or engineer, I am in insurance, auto, health, liability, and life insurance.

"I am terribly sorry if I have intruded on your space. You are intensely concentrated on the design you have sketched on that napkin."

She is still a blur to Robert as he regains control of all his manly senses that just went south of his body. The poker face begins to fade away, his hearing returns.

She turns her head again to look Robert in the eyes once again.

"May I ask, what are you drawing?"

Robert slowly regains his composure, no longer a stiff statue. His brain is coming back from a self-induced hypnotic trance. Brain cells activate in numbers. He mumbles under his breath, not yet in full mechanical control of his lips. He attempts to form coherent words, falling short of proper pronunciation. Only a few slurred words produced a response to her question. Realizing he is still not at full mental capacity to communicate.

"Damn those two glasses of scotch!" he thought.

They are preventing his speech pattern from forming audible sounds she may comprehend.

As his stare subsided, he speaks coherently for the first time.

"I do not believe I know you. Let me introduce myself. I am Robert, Robert Killings jr."

Returning the rocks glass to the bar top, Robert uses an extra napkin to dry his cold damp hand, politely extending his arm presenting his cold frozen hand in a professional manner to introduce himself to this beautiful woman sitting beside him.

"Pleased to meet you Robert, Robert Killings Jr. Do you always introduce yourself in such a manner? I mean, with a cold hand?"

Before Robert could answer, she reciprocates to Robert.

"I am Sarah, Sarah Jenkins, I seem to have startled you into a cold stare. I do apologize. I promise I am not Medusa, daughter of Phorcys and Ceto."

"Forgive me please. This is not my normal modus operandi. Although I am curious as to what it is you have on?" asks Robert.

Sarah, pausing for a moment to digest Robert's questioning.

{She hears her own internal voice}.

"Did I not fully understand his question? He is asking me what I have on?"

Deciding to play along and give it her best answer.

"It is a red Givenchy blouse. Why do you ask?"

Robert's mind was still in a fog of recovery and replied as quickly as he could.

"Sorry I was not referring to the clothing you are wearing. I smell a wonderful fragrance that has allured my sense of smell to you being the source."

Sarah felt she might be at fault for not interpreting the question and decided to slow herself. Taking another sip of wine, finishing the contents of the long stem glass, raised it to signal the bartender she was ready for another.

Here comes that inner voice in her head.

"I hope he is a man who can manage a woman that drinks a glass or two of wine, it would be bad judgement on his part, if he did have convictions or concerns."

The voices subside as she accepts the new glass of malbec. Sarah begins slowly turning her head towards Robert. He is already looking at her. Now they engage in intense eye contact. But Robert's eyes move first, discovering every inch of her face, the make-up, her cheeks down to her lips perfectly glossed.

His heart rate was climbing as he took a deep breath. Sarah begins to speak; Robert hears a lite whisper of sound as his eyes begin witnessing her lips forming words. The volume increases steadily; the audio of her voice increases in his ears to normal levels.

"It is Maison Francis Kurkjian. Do you like it she questions?"

Robert decided he could not let this woman get away from him.

"Man, up you wimp" said a voice in his head.

"I believe I would like your phone number and yes, the aroma of this fragrance is now on my list as well."

Robert Killing's life changed forever as Sarah and Robert enjoyed a good laugh. Then they began typing each other's contact information into their respective phones.

Robert and Sarah finished a lengthy conversation. Stepping out of the club, the air had become strikingly cooler.

Robert, being the gentleman, slipped off his jacket and wrapped it around Sarah's shoulders.

"My jacket should keep you warm as we walk."

"Oh, you are quite the gentleman Mr. Killings." A breath of fresh air. I could get, used to this."

This is New York city, you either grab a cab or walk the necessary blocks to your residence.

"No cab tonight if that is ok with you Sarah? Walking will give us more time to talk." said Robert.

Sarah could only provide a smile with approval then replied.

"My condominium is only a few blocks away."

The walk was slow and paced as neither wanted to rush. Sarah turned to Robert to give him instructions.

"Turn right at the next intersection, it's not far from there."

Robert agreed, continuing his stride next to Sarah. A humbled enjoyable feeling surrounded them both.

"How far now?" asked Robert.

"Another right turn at the next intersection." whispered Sarah.

The walk continued with right turns. Always a right turn.

Robert stops their stride, finally turns to look at Sarah.

"I am sure you are aware we have been taking these right turns around the same block three times now. returning to the same residential tower."

Sarah began to giggle.

"I was wondering how long it would take you to catch on. I did not think you wanted to stop talking and go home."

"Here is your jacket. I live here" as she points to the marble steps leading to a beautiful entry.

Robert took a moment to digest the significance of the Architectural design of the entryway. Again, it takes too much time to reply to Sarah.

"Are you going to stare at the building Robert or say good night?

Robert snapped out of his thoughts with Sarah's question.

"It was a pleasure to walk with you and just for the record, I was fully aware of the extra time we were taking circling the same block. Honestly, I could walk with you around the block a few more times."

Both Sarah and Robert stood for a moment gazing into each other's eyes. Robert was a gentleman. He did not want to scare Sarah away. Reaching out with the same professional courtesy for a good night handshake. Neither Robert nor Sarah wanted to be the first to let go of the others hand. That moment sealed the start of a relationship.

Robert slowly relaxed his grip on Sarah's hand. Her small soft touch would linger for the time it took to say good night. It is as if she had never let go.

"Time will pass quickly enough for the two of us. Let us continue seeing each other and decide if we are on the same path," said Robert.

"Agreed replied Sarah; I like a slow pace myself."

"The seconds of time that have passed are gone forever. The seconds to come are the most important, use them wisely for they too will be gone soon enough."

The learned experiences of past relationships will set your pace for the next one to come along. What they both wanted was a serious partner to set goals of commitment. Not a one-night stand or a game player. Agree to build a friendship with trust first and progress from there.

Sarah

Sarah had the beauty and the brains to carry herself against the best of men in her field of expertise. Many times, she had to use her quick thinking to set the record straight. Her female colleagues admired her ability to engage with people of all kinds. Everywhere she traveled, she was in command of her surroundings.

Her radiance filled a boardroom to a ballroom. There were no shortage of men challenging each other for her attention. Thwarting off many proposals, she made it clear she had no desire to settle down to be a stay-at-home spouse or simply date long term. Sarah knew from childhood she was exceptionally beautiful.

Preferring a pair of jeans and a non-revealing blouse or a dress that gave her curves brought more than enough attention. No need to display what she already knew. For now, she lived her life like she wanted, leaving the sexy babe routine to gold diggers needing a sugar daddy. She felt there would be a need for a relationship when the time was right, knowing there was no point rushing into a relationship. For now, she was in control, her life was hers, no one needed to apply for residence with her.

Her brown shoulder length hair had a silken glow that enhanced her green eyes. They were the gates to her soul. "Look me in the eyes dammit" was her motto. Catching many a man admiring her tight hourglass curves with natural breasts, there was no need to enhance them. A handful was enough for any man anyway. Smooth soft skin void of body art of any kind, in any place on her body, it was not necessary to permanently mark a specimen of her caliber.

Men would enter her life briefly. When they got close, she would announce she was leaving for an assignment with a promise to return, then ghost them forever. Sarah had yet to meet a man with the intelligence or pedigree large enough to win her heart. A man needed to be a visionary, a professional or as equal to her as possible. There would be no compromise to her principles.

Sarah needed direct access to continue as an investigative journalist. She relished the thought that one day her charming prince would appear before her when she least expected. She was a proud woman with an established career as an investigative reporter for the New York Times. Traveling around the globe researching assignments. Her mission was to procure accurate information from a range of sources, mostly requesting anonymity.

She interviewed dignitaries, congresspeople, heads of state or secret operatives. “Follow the money or the lies,” said her publisher. Sarah met anyone in any situation if they proved to possess reputable, detailed information that could be used for publication. She would stare into the souls of criminals locked up in high security prisons or travel far away into the unknown. Nothing could deter her from asking questions that could end her life.

Following a lead, she found herself in Guatemala. The assignment: meet with a low-level up and coming drug lord want to be, who was terrorizing a community. Sarah and her camera crew found themselves blindfolded in the back of an old SUV.

It was hot in the jungle. She could feel sweat dripping down her chest. Dust filled the inside of the vehicle with the windows rolling down. Of course there was no air conditioning on this mission. The old clunker bounced her and the camera crew back and forth as they traveled at a high rate of speed across a potholed dirt road. Sarah came close to vomiting her last meal as the driver continued to smoke a filthy-smelling cigar.

The vehicles stopped deep in the jungle. Stepping out the blindfolds now removed to reveal, Rinaldo El-Caterra. The infamous drug lord she came to interview. As she suspected Rinaldo was, surrounded by bodyguards. Immediately one man approached Sarah to ensure no weapons were, brought to the meeting.

Sarah extends her hand to halt the advancement.

"Just STOP RIGHT THERE! Is this necessary Rinaldo? I am not comfortable with his guards, patting her down, especially in places reserved for private partners."

Sarah knew it was a necessary part of the process and a small price to pay to be standing toe to toe with a drug lord.

Rinaldo spoke.

"Strong woman you are, I can respect your wishes this time, besides I can see by the tight curves of you pants there's no weapons hiding in them, and I might add you are much prettier than I expected."

"I came here to ask you some questions?"

Sarah stood unwavering beside the well-toned bodyguards, all bullyish looking. Their chests crossed with belts of ammo wrapped over their shoulders as they held assault rifles loaded and ready to protect their asset. They were trying hard to intimidate her.

Sarah stood strong, not flinching a muscle. If she showed any sign of weakness at that moment. The Drug lord she came to interview would have her killed.

Rinaldo questioned Sarah.

“Is this pertaining to our drug production. Or something else? Because if it is something else, you are a dead woman and the crew member that accompanied you here as well.”

“I’m here to ask questions pertaining to your drug operations, which is all” declared Sarah.

Rinaldo could spot a federal agent in seconds. He knew they sweat constantly from the heat of South America. This woman was sweating, but not a nervous sweat. At five foot four inches tall. She was too calm for the situation.

Rinaldo began a slow steady pace, walking closer to look straight into her eyes. She was not blinking, looking around or away from him, which was a sign of weakness he despised in people. This daring and beautiful woman looked him straight in the eyes.

Sarah let her voice raise an octave.

"I am waiting for a reply to my question Rinaldo? Startling him.

A second or two had passed. Sarah's mind begins the process of producing words only audible to herself.

"Did I just seal my fate? What a mistake I have made coming here."

That moment in time shared with every brain on the planet. Nothing else matters except for your inner thoughts. You hear your words as if you were speaking to yourself. Stay in control and you succeed. If the situation controls you, it could get ugly fast.

Sarah notices the armed guards were fidgeting with their weapons, desperately looking for cover that included an escape plan. She begins a short countdown in her head. Convincing herself the mayhem was about start, from ten she is now down to four…three…two.

Rinaldo breaks his silence.

"I grant you the interview, let us sit under the canopy of the trees over here. Pointing to a large sweetgum tree. You can ask the questions you came for. Your camera operator is allowed only pictures of you and me at the table. No picture or filming of my men or this place."

“Agreed.” replied Sarah.

Barking commands in Spanish to his security team to bring chairs, a table, and a bottle of tequila.

“We drink and talk, then you go back the way you came; I will see to it you have safe passage.”

Interview concluded. Sarah and Carl, her resolute camera man again blindfolded, as the driver of the old chevy SUV cranked the engine.

Out of the dense foliage, they were allowed to remove the blindfolds. Carl, a man with a joyful personality sat silent next to Sarah as the SUV stopped at the airport.

Once on the corporate jet, Sarah glanced over at Carl. He was emotionally drained as he began crying uncontrollably.

“What is it, Carl? “What is wrong?”

“Honestly Sarah, which was the first time I thought we would not make it out alive.”

Sarah turned away from Carl, leaning back in the seat of the corporate jet, she replied.

“Carl, I had the same feeling.”

Sarah's career was thriving when she first stood next to Robert. He was just a stranger to her. As she examined the sketch on the napkin, curiosity pulled her to dig deeper.

She considered this skill as her life's purpose, finding answers, filling gaps, and assembling out-of-place details like a massive puzzle, piece by piece.

Her investigative style toward the unfamiliar motivates her to maintain a challenging pace. This is particularly remarkable given that newspapers typically avoided sending women into dangerous situations.

Her global assignments for work provided minimal time to foster personal relationships.

During her first walk around the block with Robert, she sensed through her intuition that he was unlike any other man she had met before.

Stepping up those marble steps to the electronic keypad, she entered her private code as the door buzzed, releasing the lock. She stopped halfway in, holding the door half open, she looked back at Robert as he turned to begin his final walk home.

Everyone has their own thoughts. At this moment, she thought.

"I wonder if he will turn around and look back? if he does, then he's worth keeping."

"Life is taking chances; a passed-on opportunity, leaves you with an empty feeling you will never forget."

Just as Sarah had hoped, Robert stopped, turning to look back at Sarah, one last time. Robert could see her peeking out halfway from the door. He smiled, she smiled, unseen by each other in the dim streetlights. To Sarah, it did not matter. All she needed to see that night was Robert, he turned around for a second look.

Sarah prepared for bed, welcoming a warm shower in the cool evening. She grabbed her book and glasses from the nightstand, plugged in her phone, and resumed reading where she left off. After the encounter with Robert earlier, she sought to calm her nerves. She had not felt this way towards a man in years. Soon, she began to doze off while reading.

Her cell phone began vibrating, Sarah turned her head to glance at her antique alarm clock. It is 1:00 am. Who would call her this late? Another assignment from the magazine. Who knows. Not wanting to discuss a new assignment late at night, she concludes it can wait till morning; besides, they can leave a message for her on voicemail. Sarah decides to take a quick glance at the phone to confirm her suspicion.

The screen showed a number that she did not immediately recognize from her contacts. For a moment, she wondered if it might be Robert calling her. She quickly sprang up and pressed the big green button to answer before it went to voicemail. Her heart was racing. Composing herself swiftly, she answered.

"Hello."

"Hello, Sarah. It is Robert. I was hoping you would answer. Listen, Sarah, talking with you tonight got me thinking. There is so much more for you than I know, and I am eager to learn as much about you as possible. If you are free tomorrow, it would please me to treat you to dinner. I am thinking Coqodaq, it is on 22nd St. 12 E. let us say 7:00 pm. Bring an appetite for Korean food.

"Let me check my calendar Robert, hold on a second."

Sarah rose from her seat, moved around the room to her desk, and rustled some papers to mimic the sound of looking at a calendar. She paused for a minute, listening silently. Robert sat patiently, waiting for Sarah to either confirm the date or excuse herself due to a conflict so they could reschedule. Sarah, however, never actually glanced at her scheduling book; she just stood by the desk, listening to Robert's breathing.

To Robert, a minute felt like forever. Then, her voice came through the speaker,

"Yes, it appears, I have nothing planned for tomorrow. I will see you then, Robert, and thank you for calling."

After a brief pause, she added,

"Robert, how did you know Korean food is my favorite cuisine?"

"I did not, but I do now. Good night, Sarah."

Sarah and Robert met at the restaurant and engaged in an hour-long conversation. Robert was fascinated by her journalistic endeavors. Her captivating stories left him eagerly anticipating each detail. He was impressed by her skill in integrating extensive investigative resources for her publisher.

Robert shared his adventures of flying around the country. He knew his new friend had her own experiences of various destinations across the globe. Keeping these stories on a short leash. He began describing his dream of a new corporate office at an undecided location. Sarah, with her journalist background, listened carefully to his tales of solo travel and the American culture he had experienced.

Robert asked his new companion if she would consider taking a flight with him.

"I realize you have been on several assignments that afforded you the privilege of visiting unique places, albeit dangerous at times. If you were to choose a place of travel, what destination would you select for a personnel visit to enjoy outside of an assignment?"

Sarah, being the cautious woman, she simply replied,

"I will think on that and let you know, right now let's work on us first before we start traveling together."

As the rendezvous continued. It was becoming apparent to them both, something was happening between them. Stronger feelings were coming out. A simple good night kiss was not enough. Stepping up to hold hands in public, sitting next to each other on a park bench inside central park. Sarah would lean over to Robert, placing her head on his shoulder.

Sarah would soon be a part of Roberts life. They began taking weekend trips together, visiting places Robert had previously flown into. Sarah enjoyed his ability to be her personnel tour guide everywhere they went. He knew the history and culture of the people that colonized each destination. No detail left out. Robert's knowledge was his aphrodisiac; he was a walking encyclopedia of information. It was on one of the first trips she felt comfortable enough to allow Robert to make love to her for the first time.

Her charming prince had arrived as Robert Killings Jr.

Prince charming was Roberts new nickname. To her he was indeed a charming man. One of the most intelligent men she had ever had the opportunity to meet. Especially the way she met him.

Destinations

Sarah had all but moved in with Robert, although. still maintaining her condominium as a backup plan, she never had to use it. The relationship between them had grown into a solid bond of feelings. Robert and Sarah grew inseparable.

Robert wanted her to see the same beauty of the United States he had spent so much time visiting while searching for the perfect spot to move Killings insurance agency. He began requesting Sarah accompany him on his flights. Robert was eager to have Sarah as a travel companion. Figuring out it was the best way to get to know her. A one-on-one travel companion. He questioned, "Did they have the same thoughts, desires, opinions? This would be the test of their commitment to being together.

Sarah loved her prince charmingly. He was a modest, talented man with strong convictions. He had the ability to manage a corporation with dignity and grace. Easily separating the rigors of weekly business decisions with personal pleasure. When most men she dated could not separate their whites from darks in the laundry. Robert never mixed the two while she was with him. A sophisticated trait she admired the most about Robert Killings Jr. When they were together. It was all about them. Nothing stood in the way.

Sarah was home one day, brimming with excitement as she thought of a new destination for their next grand adventure together. She decided to infuse the planning process with a unique twist.

After a long day at work, Robert ascended to their penthouse using the private elevator. As the double doors parted, he met with an unexpected sight - Sarah had affixed a map of the world to the hallway wall.

“Robert, take a look at this, Sarah began, her voice filled with anticipation. I have a plan. From now on, this is how we will determine our next travel destination. It is a method that will prevent any disagreements. Instead of one of us making the decision, we will take turns throwing this dart at the map. Wherever it lands, that is where we will go. What are your thoughts? Do you like this idea?”

Robert was moved by her words. “Sarah,” he declared, “I cannot envision a life any different from this. The mere thought of existing without you is too overwhelming to bear. You are a breath of fresh air to me.”

"I feel the same way about you, Robert," Sarah responded, her voice echoing the depth of her feelings.

Robert looked into Sarah's eyes.

"Since this is your idea, please toss the first dart at the map."

Sarah threw the dart at the map. It landed in the middle of Germany.

"Well Robert, what do you think of Germany?"

"Actually Sarah, there is an insurance expo in Nuremberg in a couple of weeks. The company can use a tax right off and we can visit the Schloss Faber Castell and other castles that were, rebuilt after World War two."

Sarah beamed with excitement.

"I better pack extra clothes its chilly over there this time of year, better yet I need to go shopping for Bavarian outfits. I am sure you will enjoy seeing me in that sexy outfit."

"Ok Sarah this is your baby, schedule the flight and the accommodations. I will sign up for the insurance expo."

"Alright Robert, I can make that happen."

Commercial flying made Robert nervous. He was not at the controls of this 747. Boarding first class he and Sarah were close enough to the cockpit to give him some comfort he could be, called upon to take control if the pilot and co-pilot were unable to fly them safely down from Thirty-five thousand feet. He had a dream of flying one of these behemoths, although he was only certified on a small single engine plane.

Landing in Frankfurt Robert secured the rental car to drive the two of them to the Hotel Drei Rabin Nuremberg. Checking in was a breeze as the staff spoke English.

"I am going to freshen up Robert, it is always ladies first."

Robert sat on the edge of the bed. The lush comforter was already turned down for them by the housekeepers. Atop both pillows sat handmade animals formed from the white towels. A slow chuckle formed and a reminder he needed to use the restroom quickly.

"Sarah, will you hurry up? It has been a long drive, and I must use the facility."

Out pops Sarah from the toilet room. Sarah playfully replying, "all yours."

It is German culture to have separate names for the bathroom and toilet areas. You do not bathe in the toilet.

Robert entered the toilet room to relieve himself. To his right was a small rubbish can. Inside the can he could see a pregnancy tester. In Sarah's haste to exit she forgot to wrap the tester in tissue for concealment.

Robert now finished he bent over retrieving the used tester. Stepping out into the main room he could see Sarah setting her bag on one of the luggage racks. Slightly bending over from the waist Robert paused to enjoy the view of Sarah from behind her. Clearing his throat to gain her attention, she stood erectly turning toward Robert.

"Everything all right my darling? she asked.

Raising the tester in the air. He replied.

"Do we need to talk about this?"

"Oh that, no need to get excited it was negative, I missed a cycle so I thought I would take a test. It is the start of menopause instead."

"Sarah, you do know I would welcome our child if you were to be pregnant."

"Yes, my love, but it is too late in life for me anyway, enough of this, let us enjoy our time in Deutschland. Now go put that thing in the rubbish can where it belongs. We have a long weekend of sightseeing ahead of us."

With a girlish playful voice, she responds to Robert.

"Later on, tonight, I will wear that new Bavarian outfit I promised you."

"Why make me wait?"

"No quickies Robert," Sarah said with a smile and a wink.

"I will gladly wait."

Out of the Hotel, Robert and Sarah began a scenic walk down the sidewalk.

"I see these streets are all cobble stones remarked Sarah."

"Yes, they are. After the war, raw materials to build roadbeds were scarce. The only option was to continue using these river rocks for roadways. Some things should remain the same. They believe in maintaining the culture and heritage they know and love."

The walk together in Germany, provided inspiration to their relationship. It was a needy to build on their feelings if it was truly meant to be. Robert could not stop talking about the architectural designs of the German culture. Sarah enjoyed how Robert could get inspiration from an object's natural design. He could see a use for everything in its natural form. She once envisioned he possessed the mind of Albert Einstein. His talent and his intelligence.

One final evening in Nuremberg, Robert and Sarah were dining on fresh fish at Fisch Kuche Picklesimer. Robert sat listening to Sarah describing details of her past assignment. As she began giving her presentation. Robert slipped into the state of mind we all are guilty of.

No sound but his own thoughts as he watched his beautiful Sarah begin talking and describing the details of her interview. Robert now locked onto her beautiful face. Her hair was magnificent, her cheeks were slightly red, her lips were so inviting he stood up from the table. Placing his napkin on the armrest of the chair, then he walked around to Sarah's side of the table.

Instantly noticing Robert was beside her. She stopped talking. Looking up at Robert with a puzzled face, she sat still, as Robert gently reached under her chin, slowly lifting it upward as he bent down to give her his best enthusiastic kiss. Then releasing her to her thoughts as her head still tilted upward.

Without a word spoken by Robert, he returned to his seat.

"You were saying my love, please continue."

"Robert, Thank you for that. It was so sweet."

Robert broke from the moment by announcing.

"I have to go the restroom darling; I will be right back."

Sarah was, never shocked at the way Robert could still her with his touch as she playfully replied.

"Thanks for the kiss 'ahead' of your absence to the boy's room. It is much better to be kissed before and not after your return. Knowing what your hand had been touching."

"Always my love," Replied Robert.

Robert returned to the table. Sarah was all smiles. Her charming prince had returned to her.

Sarah looked at Robert. Playfully raising her eyebrows, she asks Robert.

“Are you ready to see the skimpy Bavarian outfit I bought to wear for you?”

“You failed to include the word ‘skimpy’ when you declared you purchased the outfit.”

“Well, I hope you did not think I planned to wear it in public my love.”

"You never cease to amaze me, Sarah," as he stood and took her hand. They left the restaurant and walked to the hotel, ignoring the clerk's greeting. Practically rushing to their room, Robert's anticipation grew, fueled by Sarah's playful nature.

Sarah had Robert right where she wanted him to be at this moment.

Placing the electronic key to the electric lock. The green light emitting a go signal to Robert. He turned the handle as he embraced Sarah just inside the door with another enthusiastic kiss. Ripping their clothes off of each other as Robert kicked the Hotel room door closed behind them. A trail of shoes, pants, blouse, and undergarments lay for later retrieval from the door to the bedroom.

For now, they were together as one.

"Well Robert, this was a surprise. I will have to wear the new outfit on another occasion. You were too anxious to wait."

"I think the feeling was mutual, don't you agree?"

Sarah rolled over in bed to lay her head on Robert's chest.

"What matters most to me is being together with you, Robert."

After the Nuremberg trip. Robert allowed Sarah to plan the rest of their destinations. He conceded she had a knack for booking the best venues where they could role play with greater intimacy. Sarah was proving to be the best partner a man could ever want or need in his life.

Sarah planned a trip to Greece including the Southeast of Europe.

"Robert" Announced Sarah, I love this place. Athens is so beautiful. I wish we could live here. Don't you?" he asked with playful delight in her voice.

"Someday, in retirement. I think it would be a wonderful place for both of us to live out our elder days together." Said Robert.

Sarah stepped into the dressing room of the Airbnb they rented for the week. Standing in front of a full-length mirror. Admiring her own beauty. Her thoughts consumed her for a moment as she heard her own inner voice speak to her.

"I love this man so much. I wonder if he will ever propose to me. My heart is right with him, should I start asking questions? No, that would be a sign I am desperate. I, will say yes, when that time arrives."

Sarah hears Robert call out for her.

"Sarah, Darling let's take a romantic boat ride on the Mediterranean, shall we?"

"That sounds great, give me a minute to change, I can put on a skirt and blouse. I will grab my day bag and sunscreen."

"Ok, I will meet you downstairs, I need to hail a cabbie."

Sarah was a bit shocked as Robert never left her alone. Much less, he never went downstairs ahead of her on any previous trip.

Sarah began to fume as she changed clothes and grabbed her day bag, headed towards the door. Briskly opening it stepping out of the Airbnb.

Sarah stopped her stride as she exited the doorway, greeted with the beautiful sight of a white limo parked a few yards in front of her.

Red rose petals precisely placed on the ground leading to the open door of the limousine.

Sarah cautiously stepped on the carpet of petals as moving towards the open door of the limousine.

Robert leans his head out from the open door of the limousine, as he extends his open hand in an inviting way for her to grasp.

"Come with me my special woman. I plan to be your prince charming for the evening."

Robert had pre-planned this special moment as he mentioned softly to Sarah.

"We have a sunset cruise awaiting our arrival."

Sarah leaned down and stepped into the Limousine with Robert holding her hand to steady her.

Sarah was now sitting comfortably beside her man. She could not hold back the tears of joy that began pouring from her big brown eyes.

The limousine itself, filled with vases of red roses.

Immediately her previous questionable thoughts eroded away as she embraced her charming prince.

Sarah started kissing Robert romantically on the lips, across the face, his ears and down his neck. She could not hold her emotions as she straddled Robert whispering in his ears.

“Take me Robert, right now, right here in the limo. I want you inside me.”

Hearing the commotion in the back. The driver smiled as he pushed a button to close the divider window between them, continuing to drive a few extra times around the wharf before stopping at the boat’s mooring position to offload his clients.

Exiting the limo, Robert handed the driver a couple 'C' notes for his extra time. A smile and a gentleman's nod transferred towards each other without saying a word.

Sarah exited the limo skipping the traditional eye contact or thanking you to the driver who opened the door. She adjusted her hair first then clothing as she quickly made her way towards the waiting-charted boat.

All eyes on the wharf instantly trained on this goddess of a woman, as she executed each step with precision towards the on ramp of the awaiting dinner boat.

Once aboard, Sarah's mind began deliberating once again. As all people do when they become curious. She required a verbal answer to the question in her head.

She quickly realized they were the only two people booked for the cruise.

"Robert, What a wonderful surprise my darling. You are a true romantic.

"Only the best for you, Sarah, you know how much I adore you."

Sarah smiled, speechless, she felt his warmth inside her.

The vessel's captain greeted Robert and Sarah at the top of the ramp.

An elderly Greek Captain was now inviting them to the helm for a visit. Speaking in broken English he introduced the two lovers to his crew. Each man and woman acknowledged the introduction as they relayed a brief description of their duties.

With the tour of the helm completed they were, now escorted down to the galley to meet the head chef.

Pleasantries exchanged, Chef Miguel Cantini asked Sarah in his best broken English.

"Madam, Sarah. I have for you a sample presentation of our finest local fresh caught seafood. It would please me to choose from these selections. your choice for dinner. I will prepare for you a delicious dinner."

Sarah was delighted to see the stainless-steel table adorning the amount of protein displayed for her to choose from. She wanted to taste everything on the table before her.

Halibut, grouper, shellfish, scallops, and clams with fine cuts of beef and Lamb.

Sarah looked at the awaiting staff standing at attention, ready to begin as soon as she made her selection known.

"Everything looks divine chef Miguel. May we have a small selection of white fish, scallops with a fillet, cooked medium rare on a bed of mashed potatoes. If you would add steamed broccoli, I believe we will enjoy eating this meal."

"Thank you so much for this beautiful presentation."

The chef was beaming with excitement. This woman made her decision with authority. He quickly snapped his fingers as the staff began moving about with precision.

Looking back at Sarah. Chef Miguel took a slight bow as he said.

"Your meal will be ready very soon; may I now escort you and your husband to a lovely table on deck? You do not want to miss the sunset."

Sarah heard those words loud and clear. In her head the word resonated with her 'HUSBAND!' We look married.

She decided.

"I will go with that for now."

Her thoughts realized Robert never corrected the chef. She assumed he must be in approval of being a husband.

Dinner concluded with the sound of a small three-piece ensemble playing soft jazz as the sun sets on the horizon.

Robert placed his arms firmly around Sarah's waist whispering his devotion and commitment softly into Sarah's ear.

Sarah's cheeks were beginning to hurt from the large smile she had on her face.

The Limo ride back to the Airbnb did not take as long as it did to get to the docks.

Entering the front door Sarah turned to kiss Robert while embracing him with a strong hug then released him as she blurted out.

"HUSBAND?" What is up with that?"

Sarah turns to walk away to the bedroom. She wanted Robert, as she reports from inside the bedroom. "Are you going to follow me or just stand out there?"

A Unique Marriage Proposal

"Due diligence provides insight into the personality of an individual. The support you need to withstand all odds of what fails in a relationship, quality time together makes it all happen."

Robert, together with Sarah, immersed themselves with more time together. The continuing short fly aways coupled with longer trips around the world to destinations neither had seen before. Being with Robert anywhere was satisfying for her.

Robert began planning their next adventure immediately.

Robert again climbed into the cockpit seat as Sarah settled into her co-pilot seat next to Robert.

"Sarah, are you ready to take off? this flight is over water."

Robert, preoccupied with startup procedures; he had not noticed Sarah's attire. Looking over Sarah he could not contain his laughter. It was not her first flight that concerned her. They have been everywhere to the Cessna Citation CJ4. B.

Nestled in the copilot's seat was this strikingly beautiful woman wearing a life preserver too large for her feminine frame. Attached to the PFD was a two-way radio, an EPIRB (emergency-position indicating radio beacon), with a water activated strobe light.

Robert could not stop laughing.

"What is all this Sarah?"

"Stop laughing at me!" she cried out. Robert, I know we have flown over the Ocean on commercial airlines before, but this is different, I am prepared for anything, you know that bout me."

Robert could not help but feel love for Sarah's preparations. He had to ask her.

"I see you are prepared for ditching in the Atlantic Ocean."

"You should know me by now Robert; I am always prepared."

"This flight is a short distance over the Atlantic Ocean to the Island of Abaco."

Sarah was noticeably nervous; all she could say was.

"Please do not laugh anymore. "Water scares me, and I can't swim anyway."

"What? Almost two solid wonderful years with you by my side and I'm now learning this about you?"

Robert was surprised to hear her declaration as he commented over the microphone on the headset.

"SERIOUSLY, YOU CANNOT SWIM?"

Robert adds.

"This will be an interesting flight, Sarah."

Sarah began to pout. She was scared.

Quick thinking Robert sensed she was overwhelmed. Being the gentleman, he was. Robert reached over to hold Sarah's hand to let her know it would be all right. She looked up at Robert. Her brown eyes glistening back at his assuring smile. No words were needed at that moment, Sarah knew she was well cared for and gave Robert's hand a tight squeeze and a slow shake. This moment was his way of showing; he cared for her.

Robert purchased the small house on the Island of Abaco as a getaway in the warm sultry Bahamas as a surprise. It was a small cottage on stilts overlooking a tiny lagoon. The front porch facing Eastward to watch morning sunrises while drinking coffee before the heat of the day became unbearable. Then retreating inside for special activities of enjoying the closeness of each other.

Robert finally spoke.

"Sit back and let me tell you about the commonwealth of the Bahamas. It is an Island country within the Lucayan Archipelago of the Atlantic Ocean, it consists of more than three-thousand islands, cays, and islets. It is located North of Cuba and East of the Florida Keys."

"I love the Florida Keys Robert; can we go there after this trip?" Sarah asked.

"Did you pack enough clothes? I can fly us straight there when we finished this weekend. We can visit Hemmingway's place and a museum. I have always wanted to have a cocktail at the old bars down there, then visit the Southernmost point of the United States."

"I don't think I have enough clothes with me for that long of a trip away from home."

"Then we will plan that excursion for another time."

With the weekend now complete. The final task of loading their luggage in the lower cargo storage compartments of the plane. Donning their respective headsets Robert began the pre-flight checklist as the engine roared to life.

Taxied the plane line up with the runway. Final clearance was received from the control tower that proved the runway was now vacated.

The tower responded with final authorization. A light smile appeared across Roberts lips when he hears the Bahamian voice in his headset.

"You go now Mawn, fly away now."

Robert throttled up the engine as the Cessna propeller grabbed air, thrusting it behind them propelling the plane forward, increasing its speed to the end of the runway. Beginning to ascend to FAA regulation altitude Sarah and Robert were, now headed home too.

"The Hill."

A reference to an old saying maritime captains used to inform the crew, when the fishing ended for the day.

Back home in South Carolina Robert taxis the Citation to the hanger. Sarah relieved the flight went well and they were safely back home on U.S. soil. Unbuckling from her seat, preparing to step out of the cockpit door to descend to the tarmac.

"Sarah"

Robert shouts above the engines as they wind down.

"WHAT?" she replies.

"Sarah darling, you can take off the PFD now. Wearing that on the tarmac is out of style for such a beautiful woman."

"Oh really, WATCH THIS!"

The Citation steps unfold and with pride in her step Sarah exits the plane, one step at a time down the stairs on to the tarmac, walking with her head held high as if traversing a runway in high heels with the composure of a high-end supermodel. Still wearing the P.F.D. and assorted emergency attachments.

The ground crew staired in amazement. The Earth stood still as Sarah proceeded to walk to her awaiting car.

Robert was barely able to keep his composure, shaking his head in disbelief. His aviator friend, David Givens, joined him, standing shoulder to shoulder.

David leaned in and whispered.

"You have found a gem in her, Robert. How did you strike such luck?"

"I'm not sure."

Robert confessed, "I can only hope she feels the same about me as I do about her."

"I'm certain she does," David reassured him. Then asked. "How was your trip to Abaco, Robert?"

"Fantastic, David. In fact, I have decided to propose to Sarah."

"Congratulations, Robert! I'm sure you want this to be a memorable moment, something she'll never forget."

"Absolutely, it has to be a special moment we both will never forget."

David thought for a moment and replied.

"I have just the plan you need; I have some friends at the golf course who would be thrilled to help. I promise you; she will remember this day forever."

"That sounds great, David. But I do not play golf. Let us get this plane in the hangar, pull out a couple of chairs, sit under the wing, then you can tell me all about your plan. I could use a scotch right about now."

Sarcastically David agrees.

"I second that: especially after watching Sarah strut across the tarmac with a P.F.D. around her neck."

Both burst into laughter, struggling to contain their composure.

Sitting comfortably in folding stadium chairs, each with a cocktail. Robert joined Davids's glass with a distinctive clink.

"Cheers my friend now, tell me the brilliant idea you have, David."

"Alright, Robert, here's my idea."

After a few hours of discussion Robert listened intently then offered to tweak Davids's plan as they poured another drink.

Finally, the terms and conditions now agreed upon, the plan was set in motion.

"Sarah will never see it coming, we will make it special, no worries." Replied David.

The first part was to take Sarah on a normal routine flight. Nothing special. Robert would pretend he wanted Sarah to accompany him on a flight to view a business deal he had in the works. It was all she needed to know.

The special day had finally arrived. Robert informed Sarah to prepare for the flight over a parcel of land he was considering.

Sarah, not very eager to go flying on this day, was dawdling in her preparations.

Robert was growing impatient.

"Sarah, are you ready? We need to leave for the airport asap."

Sarah volleyed a few questions to Robert. She had no clue what Robert had planned for this flight.

"Coming my darling, I am ready, let us go. What is with the rush today? Where are you taking me anyway? Are we stopping for lunch? I have not had breakfast yet and I am getting hungry."

"I mentioned before, I have a land option I am considering. The best way to look at it is from the air. You know I always have you as my consultant when I am considering a purchase. Sarah, you can put the P.F.D. back in the closet. There is no water involved for this flight."

Sarah, relieved to hear this from Robert, profoundly replied.

"OK."

Upon their arrival at the airport Sarah noticed the Jet was still in the hanger.

"What Plane are we flying in?" she asked.

"I have secured my friend David's 1979 Mooney single engine prop for this trip."

"Wait, what? You never fly in an experimental craft. Why are we doing this? You do not trust anyone who builds this unstable experimental garage designed paper planes. Those are your words, not mine."

"NOT MINE! "ROBERT"

"Please have trust in me. This is a very stable, well-built machine by a reputable manufacturer. It is not experimental. It was specifically made for recon work from the skies. A good many of my aviator friends have them. It is safe, now please climb in."

Sarah is hesitant and asks.

"Are you sure about this?"

"Yes, my love, please climb in."

Taking off in the Cessna was like riding a bike to Robert. But the old Mooney was a different flying machine, although he was well versed and experienced to fly vintage craft.

His friend David provided insight into its character traits. She was a stubborn old gal that required more muscle to fly than brains. Gaining altitude, setting course directions they were on their way.

Both sat quietly while listening to light chatter in their headsets from other aviators flying in proximity to them. Keeping a visual awareness, it is the pilot's job to look out for other planes in your vicinity.

This is where the mind is in constant cognitive awareness of the person's surroundings. You begin an elevated state of thinking unlike your personal thoughts or debates where you are unaware of space and time. Flying is a heightened state of awareness.

Robert began to speak into the mic of his headset.

"We are going to fly North for a little while and look for Davids's country club. He is playing in a tournament today. He requested we do a fly by and wave wings at him and his friends. This will give him confidence we got this bird off the ground in one piece."

Sarah looks over at Robert.

"IN ONE PIECE! You said One piece?"

Sarah again replied with another convincing higher octave in her voice.

"That is not what I wanted to hear today, ROBERT! Promise me you will not get too crazy flying this paper plane."

Robert detected a little sarcasm in her voice and chuckled to himself.

Robert entered the coordinates for the Golf course and began to speak to Sarah headset to headset.

"Sarah, we have been together for almost two years now, would you agree we are a compatible couple?"

"Absolutely Robert, I wouldn't change anything," she declared with kind enthusiasm. Adding the normal "I love you" at the end of her reply.

The Mooney was quickly approaching the pre- programmed Coordinates...

Robert could see the golf course coming into view and began a slow left-hand turn to line up with the 18th green. A long 545-yard par five finishing hole was now below them. Leveling off and descending to one thousand feet. Sarah could hear Robert's voice stumbling; he was choking on something. Robert, she yelled into the microphone of the headset.

"ARE YOU OK?"

"Yes, I am fine, I need to ask you something, but I am a little choked up. Can you look out the window down at the course and tell me what you see?"

"Ok"

Sarah was a little confused at Robert's request but knew they were flying over a property he had in mind to purchase. Slowly she turned away and looked out the window of the Mooney.

There on the 18th green were several golf carts coming from everywhere. Sarah stared out the window, confused at what they were doing.

Part two of the plan was now beginning to unfold. Each driver had an assigned spot on the fairway. Clearly rehearsed beforehand at David's instructions. Each driver knew just where to park on the grass to form the question Robert planned to ask Sarah.

As she sat looking out the window at the golf carts, they were all moving at a fast pace.

"Hurry up! David yelled at the drivers."

Sarah could see bold letters taped to the top of each cart. The formation began to take shape. The carts' preplanned positions formed a complete sentence.

The army of golf carts finally stopped. All lined up perfectly. In bold letters atop the golf carts.

The sentence read.

"SARAH, WILL YOU MARY ME?

Tears began flowing uncontrollably from Sarah's beautiful brown eyes. Unable to contain her emotions. She looked back at Robert as he had already retrieved the ring from the front pocket of his aviator jacket.

Robert held the ring in his fingers as silence captivated the moment. Only the sound of the prop filled their headsets. Sarah turned her head away from Robert. She needed to look out the window at the golf course one more time to confirm what she had just read. The golf carts were still there. The drivers had exited the carts and began waving at the plane. Robert's adrenaline was peaking. He quickly theorized he may have pushed their relationship to a higher level without the indicator he thought he had. Again, his inner thoughts randomly filled his head. He asked himself, was his timing off?

He concluded the resulting silence may be disastrous to their future together.

Robert spared no more seconds as they were ticking away as fast as they were arriving. He needed an answer.

"Sarah" he shouted her name in the microphone.

"Are going to say anything? Please say something!

As the words flowed from his mic to her ears in the headset,

Robert's headset came alive with her voice.

"Yes, Robert Killings Jr. my prince charming, I will Marry you. Sarah responded with clarity then turned her head towards Robert.

There in his hand, held tight with two fingers, was a beautiful diamond ring.

"Is that a ring in your hand? I cannot see well right now with these tears in my eyes."

"Yes, now will you please take it? I need both hands to fly."

The headsets came alive.

"Ground control to Robert"

It was Robert's friend David; his voice filled the headset. Robert quickly summarized David was using a handheld radio to communicate from the fairway of the golf course.

Robert, "can you read me?'

Why aviators and radio men used the terminology of

"Can you read me" always perplexed Robert. It is impossible to read a radio signal.

Responding to David, Robert replied.

"We are good to go David, she said yes."

David turned to give a thumbs up to his ground crew.

They began celebrating with joyous loud yelling and waving at the Mooney flying above them.

David now yelling at his crew over the noise they created.

"That is all boys. Now get all these carts off the fairway, there is a foursome playing through."

Turning the Mooney, Robert entered the airport's coordinates and began the return flight.

The landing was as smooth as always. Setting the plane down softly on the runway, he began to taxi to the hanger.

Sarah, realizing she needs to break the silence, offers her newly confirmed fiancé the ultimate compliment all aviators take pride in hearing.

"You sure buttered that landing."

"Thank you for the compliment, Sarah."

Sarah quickly added.

"Do not get the big head. I know this is normal for your skill set."

Robert, being grateful for her compliment, quickly responded. “Sarah, the compliment would have meant more to me without the playful sarcasm at the end.”

“Love you too.”

Beaming with smiles, they both unbuckled to exit the plane.

It was Sarah who exited the plane first, almost tearing her blouse on the door latch. She could not wait any longer to embrace the man she loved so much. Running around the front of the plane, she threw her arms around him, planting a kiss on his lips.

The kiss was the longest they could remember. Finally, I finished swapping a few slobbers. Sarah and Robert stood facing each other with the excitement of young lovers.

Sarah asked.

“Are we going to stand here forever or head home to consummate this proposal?”

"Oh! Yes, let us go home.” replied Robert.

Robert turns to the ground crew.

“You know what to do boys”?

Then grabs Sarah's hand to lead the way. They almost started running to the awaiting S.U.V.

Sarah would not let go of Roberts' hand as he drove her home. She was going to marry the man that swept her off her feet.

"I have to say, that was quite a romantic way of asking a woman to marry you, Robert. I already like the sound of my new name. Mrs. Sarah Killings."

That evening Robert started planning a new trip.

"Sarah my darling, this will be our last trip together before the vows of matrimony bond us in eternity. Planning this getaway will be different knowing we will soon tie, the knot. I would like to hear your thoughts on it."

Sarah replies.

"I have been thinking we should stand down on trips until we conclude the wedding plans, then our honeymoon will mean so much more to us."

"I like your way of thinking. I will table this plan and work on our Honeymoon trip."

Roberts internal voice began to speak to him. Acknowledging this is the very reason he fell deeply in love with Sarah. Marriage to her was ideal as he could not bear the thought of living another day or any day without her by his side. They were going to be spouses forever.

Robert and Sarah shared common thinking in approaching the challenge of wedding preparations. Each detail combed over in length, checked, and double checked. Agreeing on a cake, guest lists, invitations, photographer, venue, caterer, bridesmaids, and his best man. Absolutely everything planned out together.

Except her dress. That she kept from him until the wedding day.

Sarah collected her entourage of besties for the process of picking the perfect dress. Sarah's S.U.V. was, loaded with the girls as they drove to Elizabeth Cole Bridal, in Columbia, South Carolina. The free wine helps calm the nerves as Sarah parades several elegantly prepared gowns in front of the waiting team of judges she assembles for this special moment.

To Robert it was merely another suit and tie for him and his close friends consisting of business professionals and aviator fly boys. Sarah did mention he should buy a new pair of shoes though. It was the easiest part of the whole ordeal.

Robert married Sarah in St. Joseph's Catholic church. With the ceremony and reception completed. They headed home to pack for the honeymoon.

Robert not wanting to leave the United States, made reservations in Ashville, North Carolina at the Omni Grove Park Inn.

His plan was to pamper his now wife with the excellence of amenities offered at the resort. Sarah was treated to facials and massages. Robert accompanied her daily for poolside cocktails. Holding her hand as they lounged in the warm sun.

Evenings were reserved for dining in the finest cuisine Ashville had to offer. They retired to their honeymoon suit every night to embrace each other with the enthusiastic love of teenagers.

Robert asserted to Sarah his commitment to her would never falter. She would never have to worry about anything while they were together.

"One last request my darling, now that we are joined together."

“Anything for you prince charming”

“I think it is time you part ways with your apartment in New York, do you agree?”

“Agreed” I do not need it anymore.”

Returning to Columbia, South Carolina, Robert now informed the lead fraud investigator had resigned his position to return to his hometown of New York.

Sighting her reason for family was deeply rooted and missed her.

Robert began the process of finding a replacement for this resolute employee that had started as a young lady doing minor clerical work for his father. Promotion after promotion secured her to the highest-ranking position as lead fraud investigator.

Robert needed someone with the same caliber mindset to supervise the mass of employees of the fraud division.

Killings insurance LLC was a diverse divisional company that provided policies that protected business liability with large and small assets, an automotive division, health, and welfare policies including small and extremely large life insurance policies.

The vetting process began immediately. A local staffing agency failed miserably in their efforts to send a competent qualified candidate.

The board chose to contract out the search process with a recruiter.

Not a single person was available or found qualified for the position.

Robert was at a loss for the first time as C.E.O. It was a Friday evening. Pouring his Favorite Dewars over a large single cube of ice. He sat on the leather sofa staring out the windows at the skyline night lights of Columbia, South Carolina.

It was another aspect of his design. The windows were floor to ceiling that stood as a barrier to the Southern heat of South Carolina.

The sound of the Elevator door opens, and Sarah enters the suite and began reporting aloud to Robert.

“Hey babe, I have been at the gym with some girlfriends. How is your day today?”

Robert is deep in thought, not realizing Sarah was speaking to him. She stops walking behind him. Turns to look at him. This is strange behavior from her man. Sarah stood for a second. Her mind deliberated. This silence from Robert will not be tolerated. He always recognizes her entrance and is still staring out the window.

She asks with a stern commanding voice.

"Are you going to answer me Robert? what is wrong? You do not look good, and you have not recognized my entrance as you always do. You look worried."

"Oh! Sarah my darling I did not hear you come in."

"I see that."

Sarah walks around the sofa to face him.

Robert looks up to see Sarah has placed herself in front of him.

"Please sit with me?" he asks.

Robert begins the conversation regarding employee retiring.

Robert has always shielded Sarah from business or expressing any problems he encounters with the company. He now needed the advice of his companion. For he was now faced with a compounding problem of finding a replacement for a resolute employee.

Robert begins his conversation with Sarah.

"It is getting difficult to replace a good employee. The headhunters and local staffing agencies have come up empty."

Sarah slips off the sofa and places herself on her knees in front of Robert. Reaching out to Robert's face with her soft and gentle hands, bringing his face close to hers, giving him a kiss.

Still holding his face while looking him in his eyes. She releases her hold onto him and speaks with a full joyful tone.

"I can do that job."

Robert melts when she does that. She is irresistible.

Sarah continues.

"The Times have not sent me on an assignment in months since we got married. Either they are giving me time to adjust to married life, or they have forgotten about me."

Robert could not believe Sarah would entertain having a desk position, but he was now desperate to fill the open spot.

"Ok then you can start Monday, you are perfect for the job anyway."

Sarah would soon start working in her new career as head of the fraud investigation department.

"It can be temporary if you want, I know your rules of family working at the company and the need to have respect for any position at the company."

Robert declared.

"I will happily break my own rule for you, my love."

The Last Flight

"There's that annoying phone ringing again'" Sarah, please answer it. Tell them you are not interested in another assignment and please inform your superiors of your intentions to submit your resignation. You have accepted a position at Killings insurance."

Sarah reluctantly picked up the phone after the third attempt by someone intent on contacting her.

"Hello, yes, this is Sarah Killings" "Sure I can, Texas? Did you say."

The caller began detailing her assignment. Head to Texas. A drilling team had found a hidden deposit if oil reserves deep beneath the Gulf of Mexico. The company had discovered a cache so rich it would dwarf the O.P.E.C. production statistics for years to come. If the story were to break open before the market investors had a chance to analyze the data. It could be problematic. Sarah was to be discreet about the details of her findings. The assignment carried strict rules of confidentiality. No one is to know her discovery.

The markets open on Monday. She was to leave now and get to Galveston, Texas.

Robert was entering the kitchen where Sarah was standing. Setting down her cell phone, looking up at Robert.

"Sorry dear, I need to take this one last assignment and then I promise you, I will tell them I'm finished; I will resign my position."

"I must go to Galveston, Texas" right away, this is a hot story."

"What is this one about?" Robert asks.

"Unfortunately, I cannot discuss it without compromising you with insider information. Acting on it can cause problems, and we cannot have the Securities and Exchange commission investigating you or me. It will be public information on the 6:00 o'clock news on Monday evening after the markets close."

"What are your plans for today? Are you going flying after working out?" Asked Sarah

"I plan to go to David's hanger house, they have a runway right outside the back door, a one plane strip for take-off and landing. He has two planes in a hanger attached to the small living quarters. We are going up in one of them today. And fly to Greenville, South Carolina for lunch. We may get grounded if afternoon thunderstorms roll in. I can call to cancel with him if you want to spend some time together before you leave, or I can drive you to the airport?"

"No, I can grab a cab. You and David have an enjoyable day flying. We are close to Columbia Metropolitan airport anyway. It is a one-day round trip. The Magazine's corporate jet has just arrived from New York, re-fueled and is waiting for me to get on board."

"I have my day bag on standby. Kiss me good-bye my love, I will return later tonight."

Robert pulled Sarah in close, wrapping his arms around her tiny waist. His hands slipped down her back as his strong hands grabbed her bottom, pulling her close to him. She could feel his appendage wanting her through his thin polyester work out pants.

"Must you leave, RIGHT THIS MINUTE?"

"Robert my love, this will have to wait until tonight. I cannot be flying all the way to Texas soaking wet with your love juices between my legs. I promise to make it up to you tonight."

"Bye now."

Sarah presses the button that opens the private elevator door. The elevator doors are still open as she turns to look at Robert.

"Have a great day flying and stay out of those paper planes."

Robert broke into a smile as he watched the elevator doors close in front of his beautiful Sarah.

A Short ride down, she is at street level to meet the awaiting limousine the magazine sent to retrieve her.

Robert knew exactly what she meant. Experimental planes gave him cause for concern. So many were unproven designs. His experience of losing close friends along with other aviators to the failure of the home-built contraptions.

While Sarah was off to Texas. Robert finished a short workout and, like Sarah an hour before him, stepped into the elevator, turned to watch the doors close, beginning its descent into the secure parking level.

It was a short drive to David's hanger home located an hour from downtown Columbia South Carolina. Robert, listening to the radio playing classic rock and roll had drifted into the familiar trance of self-thinking. The music was no longer entertaining his ears.

Robert was in full internal thinking mode, listening to himself instead of music on the radio. Robert's thoughts are of Sarah. How could I get so lucky to find her? The first time his eyes met hers in that club, that night and the walk home will always stay tucked away as a memory. There are certain meaningful events we never fully lose contact with when in our inner thinking mode. The music changes as Robert makes the turn in the small air park bringing his inner thinking back to the reality of cognitive awareness. David's Hanger home looked like an oversized double wide modular home. A big, long-slope roof covered two small planes sitting comfortably beside each other next to the main house structure.

Spotting David working on one of the two planes. Robert parked the car and stepped out to greet his friend.

Handshake's complete, they began to discuss the options of the day flying adventure.

"Which one of these two beauties are we going up in today?" asked Robert.

"I have been assembling this two-seater kit plane, and it is ready for a trial run, would you be interested in being my copilot for the initial shakedown?

"David, you are fully aware of my opinion on trial runs of experimental airplanes, even if you have flown the dam thing a hundred times, I will not consider it."

"Robert, in all honesty do you think after all these years of being a close friend of mine, I would put you or my-self for that matter up in a plane I did not have confidence in?"

David continued to ridicule Robert and evaluate his maturity.

He continued.

"I am tired of you being a wimp, Robert. We are going up in this plane. It also aggravates me, how you have never put trust in me or my ability to build these things. You have known me for a long time. They always fly. I have never failed to get back on the ground. So, quit being a puss."

The man code between friends was at stake, Robert was not going to be, humiliated and called a "puss'" He im-mediately replied to David.

"Sarah will never forgive me if I do this, and if this ends on a sour note there will be hell to pay when I get home, she knows me well. Sarah reminded me to stay out of the pa-per airplanes as she stepped in the elevator this morning."

David stopped to answer Robert.

"Elevator? Is she off on another one of her dangerous assignments?"

"Yes, she left just before me on assignment to Texas, in fact, under strict requirement of confidentiality on this one. I will get details when she returns tonight. I swear David, I really believe she could be a spy for the C.I.A. that pretends to be a journalist to cover up her real identity."

"Well then Robert, she is not here to hold your hand or grab you by the ear and trot you home for a whipping like your momma used to do."

"Robert, you are a grown man, grow a set will you for once in your life? Man-up and get in, what was that quote from your dad? Life is taking chance."

Robert immediately cut David off.

"Shut your trap, which is enough David. I know his quotes all too well."

"All right," said Robert, I will saddle up. Let us get this thing in the air. Just promise me you will NEVER! speak a word of this day to Sarah. EVER!"

"Do we need to lock pinkies and sing Kumbaya before we fly?"

"Let it go, David; just let it go."

David and Robert completed the external walk around the plane checking the skin, inspecting the prop, kicking the tires making sure the air pressure was correct, then climbed in and secured themselves in the seats as Robert gave his seatbelt a little extra tug to secure himself.

David began the preflight checklist. Grabbing the control stick, rotating it to check how the flaps reacted to its position. Working them up and down, now using the foot controls to move the rudder side to side.

David continued operating the system checking every detail that would effectively manage the plane's aerodynamics to maneuver where and how he wanted the plane to fly.

Robert was uniquely impressed with David's ability to build this flying machine by himself. He had a talent for mechanical engineering he knew nothing about.

Placing the headsets on their ears, David began to speak.

"Ok, Robert I think we are all set to take flight and see what this baby can do."

Reaching flying speed at the end of the grass runway. David's creation took flight as a sigh of relief swept over Robert.

"I feel like the Wright Brothers, David."

Finally leveling off at two-thousand feet, they hear the sound that penetrated the otherwise soundproof headsets. Headsets are engineered to block dangerous outside noise and protect the ears.

"David, did you hear that?"

Robert looks over at David, he is in a frantic attempt to gain control of the plane.

"NO STICK" yelled David

"I have lost control of the flaps."

The plane is descending fast.

Below them was interstate 20 that traverses across South Carolina.

"Can you set down on the interstate?" Robert quickly asked.

"Oh, we are heading to the interstate alright, only problem is we are heading into oncoming traffic," said David.

"David, DAVID! do you see the 18-wheeler coming at us?"

David is silent. He is still frantically trying to regain control of the plane.

Robert knew the plane was losing power.

David Yelled into the microphone. "DAMMIT! We must have bad fuel on top of everything else."

"No time to say goodbye is what funeral directors hear all too often from survivors."

The speed of decent increases rapidly. Robert and David were descending closer and closer to the oncoming traffic. Some drivers could see the approaching small plane and veered off the highway.

It became clear to them an 18-wheel truck driver was not paying attention as he should be.

Just before the impact the driver looked up at the approaching plane looking eye to eye with the two occupants of the plane.

When the first smart bombs had been, developed at the end of the Vietnam war. The cameras installed in the nose of the bombs sent detailed video of the flight. It allowed an operator to correct its flight path to ensure precise impact on a target. One flight targeting a bridge showed in detail the images of the rivets embedded in bridge in the last frames of the video just before impact.

Robert could see the shock of the truck drivers face seconds before the impact. In an instant the plane embedded into the windshield.

"It was a direct impact." said the trooper working the scene.

"Anyone survive?" asked the trooper's supervisor.

"No one," replied the trooper.

Processing

The mind needs time to heal like a wound on the skin. Losing someone close to you is not only tragic but an emotional roller coaster.

The initial report of the loss is devastating. Your thoughts become scattered as you process the news. You begin with the first phase.

Denial.

The other person recalls memories. The process of questioning why occupies your thoughts for days and weeks. They can continue for longer periods up to years if you cannot process the answers you are looking for. The time it takes to accept the event is different for everyone. Some can process the loss quickly and accept it. Some turn to faith for the answers to try to move on, while others never find peace within them to forgive and forget.

Accidental loss is one example of life's tragedies. Losing a loved one in this manner starts a radical succession of thoughts. You regard the delivery of information to be untrue. Initially you cannot accept the thoughts. Your brain refuses to believe the news you have received. Once you are convinced the tragedy is real, you enter phase two.

Acceptance.

This phase is near to denial. You give way to the information received as it now becomes reality your partner is gone. During this phase you continue to think about the person as if they are in the present. Near you. You call out their name unaware of the act. Then instantly, silence overcomes you. Mere seconds afterward as your conscious mind knowingly reacts to your action. Momentarily your body functions freeze. The mind reflects on your activity.

You are motionless.

You begin with questioning. How did this happen? Then why did it have to be him / her? The due diligence begins. You become the investigator for your own thoughts. There is a plethora of unanswered questions you have floating in your brain. You need answers.

Time begins with the heeling, and you move on.

Forgiveness.

The person's mind left behind believes the loss is not their fault. After you discovered the cause of the tragedy was their fault for not taking the proper procedures to avert their departure. The phase will begin when you have had the time to find the need to move on from the other phases. An accident is an accident that nothing could have prevented it from happening in the first place.

You forgive them.

Only then can you move forward with your own life.

Relationships are the same. Just Friends, a romantic partner to married couples that experience separation or divorce. The worst is of a romantic break-up when a significant partner decides to lie about their infidelity. All of this can have a profound devastating impact on your emotional feelings for the mind to process in phases.

The intensity of each phase depends on the level of commitment and involvement of the relationship with the person you have departed from or lost.

A death is difficult enough although their memory will become fainter with time. The absence of the person will soon be removed from recalled memory allowing a path to healing as the memory of them fades away.

A breakup is the most difficult part of the phase processing. Especially with a significant other who may live in proximity to you. The departure from a normal routine relationship to a breakup may have been, caused by a workplace romance.

A visual encounter triggers the mind to retrieve the good and the bad memories of the person you loved.

You start all over again questioning why. This process of memory recall continues to be in the form of analyzing. Every bit of information to justify the existence of that person is scrutinized in the questionable form of why. This one question remains unanswered. You will never lose that one thought until you get closure.

Why did this happen?

The emotional feelings not only control your emotional thinking, but they also affect your entire bodily functions, causing a traumatic effect on a person for days and even months. You stop eating. Your demeanor is noticeable to everyone around you. Not until you find clarity in one of the phases. You will not be able to clear it from the memory of the mind.

You only move away from these debating thoughts when the mind becomes preoccupied with new memories or accepts a new challenge to your intellectual universe.

Your memories, thoughts, debates, questions need to be concluded to accept closure. Everyone processes the information in their own way when grieving the loss of a partner.

Seek closure as quickly as possible or you can be emotionally drained forever.

Where is my Robeert?

Sarah was excited to finish her assignment in Texas and return to Robert. It would be a new beginning. A new challenge to prove herself on another stage.

Investigating was her life's work; she was well respected as a seasoned professional and highly regarded as an investigative journalist. A career choice filled with mostly masculine men full of testosterone itching to prove who was better than the other.

The corporate jet was now wheeling down on the airport's runway. Sarah climbed into the awaiting limousine as the driver began the return drive to her penthouse. She was tired but knew soon she would be, dropped off at the entrance to Killings insurance office building. The thoughts of curling up with Robert circled within her mind as her pace quickened like a teenager coming home to tell her mom about a new beau.

Stepping into the private elevator. There were several buttons to select, but only four she ever used. First two for parking garage and street level. Above those were two more. One for the office floor and the bright red one for the penthouse. Finger ready, she playfully selected the penthouse.

The Elevator seemed slower than usual. Her anticipation of seeing Robert, her love.

"Come on elevator, what is taking so long?"

The annoying bell rings out as the doors slide open.

Sarah shouts out.

"ROBERT, my love, I am home, where are you?"

There was no response, no voice to hear. Not in the bedroom Nothing from the kitchen nor the living room. No Robert anywhere in the penthouse. Looking frantically for a note explaining his absence revealed nothing. Sarah retrieved her cell phone from her purse. She dials Roberts' number only to hear his phone ringing. Stepping into the bathroom to find

Robert's phone still ringing as she sees her avatar filling the glass screen.

The words resonate in her head.

"Oh, dear that man must love me to have my picture come up on his phone when I call."

Sarah naturally was not overly concerned about Robert's absence as he always lets her know when he's grounded by weather and must get a hotel.

The skies were a bit dark as the corporate jet landed in Columbia, South Carolina.

He will be back in the morning as always. She settles down too her laptop to begin the tedious task of drafting her report.

Sarah studied her notes, fingers on both hands went to work searching out key by key to comprise the words describing her interview with the drilling team supervisor and company official. This report was to be her final mission for the newspaper.

It was typing, editing, more typing, more editing. Referring to notes, listening to a voice recorder, watching videos downloaded by Carl the photographer. No source of information was ignored to author the last story of her career as an investigative journalist.

Sarah glanced at the time at her laptop and could not believe it was 3:00 am. Double checking the giant wall clock to confirm. She finished with her masterpiece. The Only thing left was to email it to the publisher for review. Sarah opened her email, selected the addressee, attached the pdf document, and sent it.

Heading to bed she thought of Robert's lack of communication. His whereabouts were unknown, she remembered he had left his cell phone, but he could have used Davids's phone. She quickly summarized how long gone the days when a person could recite a land line number from memory. All contacts now stored in a minicomputer in the palm of your hand. With these forgiving thoughts Sarah slipped under the covers, exhausted and tired, lowered her head, feeling the softness of the pillowcase. Closed her eyes, as she quickly fell asleep.

Morning was breaking. Sarah tried in vain to sleep longer than she normally does. It was not meant to be on this day. The sun rises crested the Eastern horizon, bringing with it the morning amber glow that slowly turns to daylight. The bright rays begin illuminating the bedroom. Sarah was awakening, stretching her arms instinctively for the warmth of Robert, she always scooted in close behind him, wrapping her arms over him, laying her palm on his well-toned masculine chest. Letting her tiny feminine fingers feel his chest hair. She needed him.

"Where is he?"

Rising from the bed Sarah headed to the walk-in shower. She could not help but think of Robert. All those detailed thoughts of Robert's sketches on those napkins. His thoughts were so detailed. Right down to the shower completely lined with granite tiles. Reaching in she turned the dark bronze knobs, sending a mixture of hot and chilly water to the rain head. Setting it for the right temperature she waited for the steam to form on the glass before entering.

She leaves the shower area entering the kitchen. There sitting under the hand-crafted cabinets sits the multiple function coffee maker. No espresso today, only plain coffee as she set it the machine to perk on its own.

Her mind instantly filled with the thought of Robert, and how he loved his old percolator coffee maker, he was right, it did make a great cup of coffee.

Returning to the shower, she is relieved the water is awaiting its chance to cleanse her body. Dropping her robe, she steps in and turns another valve. Multiple water jets engulf her entire body with spray from several directions.

She once again thinks about Robert.

"What a joy it is to have this man and his abilities in her life."

Sitting down at her private vanity. Sarah's begins her daily ritual of putting on her make-up for the new job. The world needed to view a pretty face.

Make up on, she pours a full cup of coffee and takes a sip of her favorite rich Columbian Dark roast. Instinctively, she reaches for her cell phone and dials Robert. Then quickly he remembers his phone ringing in the bedroom.

Sarah stops for a brief moment. She hears the words in her head.

"Where is Robert, my prince charming? This is not like him."

Sarah's phone begins to ring. Rushing to find it. She once again listens to her inner voice.

"It has to be Robert calling from another number. I hope he has a good excuse for getting her upset like this?"

"Hello Sarah" said the female voice.

"Oh, hello Charlotte how are today? Are you calling about the story I emailed you?"

"Yes I am. Let us go over the fine points before we air the report. We want to clarify every detail before it airs on the nightly news. This is big news, and we need it right the first time. I am informing you first it will be your name on this exclusive report. Would you be willing to go live with it? I can have a camera crew at your penthouse in a couple of hours for some rehearsal shooting."

"Charlotte, you know I am not comfortable in front of a camera with a live audience. The answer is No."

Sarah's phone conversation was temporarily interrupted with a second caller attempting to connect with Sarah. She briefly looks at the secondary caller ID.

It was Elanor.

Brushing it off Sarah continues talking to the show's producer, Charlotte.

"I knew you were going to say that Sarah. We are prepared to give you a nice bonus for taking the lead for us on this story if you agree to go live, we desperately want you to be the reporter for this story so please reconsider. You know how big this is going to affect our economy and the stock market once this news is, made public."

"Yes, Charlotte I do understand the implications. I just cannot do it. If I did I would not be able to fulfill my promise to Robert. You know how much I care for this man. I made a promise to resign as soon as I got the information and turned it in to you."

Sarah's phone rings once more. Again, it is Eleanor from downstairs.

"I am terribly sorry Charlotte. I am finished with investigative reporting. I must say goodbye for now; my phone is blowing up by Eleanor downstairs. I have to answer her."

"Goodbye"

As Sarah was ending her call with Charlotte the phone rang again for the third time. This time Sarah answered.

It was Eleanor calling. Sarah listened as Eleanor struggled to speak.

“Oh deer, Hello Sarah. It is Elanor from downstairs. I have a couple of gentlemen here to see you. We are entering the elevator. See you in a minute.”

Before Sarah could respond, Elanor ended the call.

Heart Breaking News

Sarah reached the elevator doors, reaching out to release the security lock for the doors, they had already begun to open. Sarah was now standing in front of two of South Carolina's finest State Highway Patrolmen. Leading them out of the elevator was their escort, Elanor, the ground floor receptionist.

A cold stern looking face is the first line of defense you encounter when passing through the doors of a major corporation.

It is always the receptionist who greets you. Elanor was German born. With the unmistaken characteristic of her heritage and stout bulldog frame. She let no one slip by her.

She stood in front of Sarah and spoke.

"Mrs. killings, um, Sarah, these gentlemen are here to see you, would you like me to stay while they speak to you?

"I do not understand Elanor. Why are they here?

I have not been driving lately. Wait a minute! has something happened to Robert?"

"I will let them explain everything Sarah, I will be right here."

Elanor stepped back to the rear of the two police officers like an armed guard as they removed their hats and stepped forward towards Sarah.

A moment of silence as everyone awaited the news from the state troopers.

No single person on earth desires to see two fully dressed state police officer arrived at your door. You know why they have come. Your body tenses, palms sweat, the nerves on the back of your neck tingle, as they begin to inform you of the passing of your loved one.

Nothing can prepare you for that moment.

Your life changes in an instant. Your emotions turn against your motor functions. A sense of frustration overcomes you as you lose the ability to control thoughts you were once in control of. Standard composure now compromised. You are helpless.

The State Troopers assigned to the task had delivered the unwelcome news and turned into the elevator. As the doors closed in front of them.

"This never gets easy," said one of them.

Elanor sat with Sarah comforting her for some time. Sarah lost the will to stand. She was now slumped on the sofa unable to move. Tears from crying, her face and blouse, they would not stop for hours to come.

The makeup she took so much time perfecting that morning in readying herself for a vibrant day in her new position was now gone from her face.

Elanor had excused herself and was now gone for the day. Promising to field all the calls that had already started pouring into Killings Insurance LLC as the news started breaking. Elanor's position was now unfolding.

Shield Sarah from the media, set up a shop in the lobby.

Sarah refused to answer the relentless questioning. Instead, she felt the need to prepare a statement for Elanor to read a short statement into a set of microphones perfectly placed in front of the news cameras.

"Today we announce the tragic passing of Robert Killings jr. The C.E.O. of Killings insurance LLC. A brilliant, honorable, loving man to his wife Sarah Killings. The board of directors will now take control of the company while they seek to elect a new C.E.O.

Our condolences to the driver of the tractor trailer involved with this unavoidable accident.

No further comment at this time. Good day ladies and gentlemen."

The next day, Elanor was encouraged to make the needed arrangements. Taking the burden off Sarah in her time of mourning.

Attending Roberts' funeral there were so many acquaintances, business professionals and world dignitaries that Sarah could not count them all. It was more than the attendance at her and Robert's wedding.

With the celebration of life complete. It was time to address the issue of who would become C.E.O of Killings insurance, LLC.

Out of respect Sarah had to be considered a valid candidate. As Roberts' last will and testament did expressly convey his wishes that Sarah was to inherit everything in the event of his demise.

Even in Roberts' passing he had every detail spelled out. If a new executive officer cannot be secured. The business needed divested and sold. It was his wish. Sarah would retain ownership of the penthouse in perpetuity.

Sarah addressed the board and confessed she was not ready to accept the responsibilities of the top position. She admitted she was not prepared or knowledgeable enough to manage the task of being C.E.O. of Killings Insurance, LLC, and requested her name be stricken from consideration.

At the same meeting Sarah requested that she remain employed with the fraud department where her education and experience would best serve the company. She conveyed it was Robert who had offered her that position.

Sarah expressed.

"Respectfully I want to be a part of Roberts legacy."

The board entertained a motion to accept Sarah as the lead investigator of the fraud department, a second then duly recorded with an immediate second to the vote. The board agreed upon the motion without debate and moved on to a more appropriate candidate.

It was also granted at the insistence of the board of directors that Sarah was to be, granted the necessary time to grieve for Robert before beginning her duties.

Sarah selected to do just that as she flew home to the cooler temperature New York as the South Carolina summer months were upon them.

Sarah was out of the office for a full month when she decided it was time to return to South Carolina.

It was time to focus on the mountain of backlog cases on her desk. Investigations with the fraud team were under a huge backlog. No one had taken the lead position of authority out of respect while she was away, and the team had been without a leader to give them direction for a month, and it was showing.

Without proper procedures implemented or follow-up on systematic yearly reviews of fraud cases. Life insurance payouts were unknowingly authorized without due process.

One such life insurance payout was enormous. Sarah opened the file and began reading the claim. She could not believe the total loss of life payout was FIFTY MILLION DOLLARS. The life insurance policy coverage was the same amount of payout for each of two sons of a man who owned a sea food processing company and a fleet of shrimp boats. He lived in Charleston, South Carolina.

The policy was, written in a manner she did not understand, the policy holder had already perished in natural causes.

But the policy payout beneficiary funds were not to be paid to the father.

Instead, the policy stated if either son perished the claim was to be, paid in full to the surviving sibling in the event the passing of the father before either son was to meet an untimely demise.

The Father had passed away some years ago from a heart attack while collecting the shrimp net back on the boat. His company had successfully continued paying the premiums on auto pay from the corporate account.

Sarah yells out from her desk at her personnel assistant.

"Carley" get in here."

Carley quickly enters Sarah's office.

"Yes Sarah, what can I help you with?"

"Get a meeting set up asap, we need to find out who signed off on this claim and authorized this payout."

Carly gathered the appropriate employees and set up a meeting with everyone involved in processing the claim.

After a grueling hour-long meeting, no one employed at the time accepted responsibility.

The meeting is now adjourned. Sarah noticed the required authorizing signatures were missing. Although a check for Fifty Million dollars had cleared Killings Insurance LLC bank account.

Sarah could not let it go. This was too much money and who wrote the policy in the first place.

"Carley," She yelled again from her desk.

"Yes Mrs. Killings"

"Stop with the formal dressing, you have been told and reminded to call me Sarah, please remember that."

"My apologies Sarah, I thought you were mad at me."

"I am handing you this case. Assemble a team of our best investigators. It will be your job to report on how this happened, and I do not care how long it takes. Find the reason this claim processed and Carley, this is our eyes only, no one else in the division or within the company is to be, consulted without my permission, GOT IT?"

"Yes Ma'am."

"You are so Southern Carley, …. Ma'am my ass"

The season was changing, and October's cooler weather crept in slowly as the southern states prepared for fall. Short pants and flip flops now replaced the long jeans and slip on shoes. Still no socks were worn as it is a Southern thing no one understands. Water sports have given way to college football and rivalries are now in full force.

Sarah immersed herself in work increasingly to ease the pain of losing her precious Robert. Catching herself bursting into tears at her desk was common. The staff had difficulty accepting the loss of Robert just as much as Sarah.

Sarah yearned for her partner. The prince charming she deeply loved was gone.

Beginning to accept her future as a widow. She found herself watching the younger girls in the division share pictures of their offspring in Halloween costumes.

Sarah and Robert did not have children. They discussed it in detail. She briefly recalls Robert's face as he exited the bathroom in Germany. Oh! The look on his face. The memory briefly brought a smile to Sarah's face with a slight chuckle.

Carly hears Sarah's chuckle. She runs into Sarah's office.

"ARE YOU ALRIGHT SARAH?"

Sarah looks up at Carley with a big grin.

"Yes, Carley I am fine."

As Thanksgiving approached a few employees offered Sarah a seat at their family dinner tables, she respectfully declined all invitations. She decided to sit out turkey day and sat at home alone, reminiscing of days with Robert and the trips together. She was not ready for cooking, drinking and parties filled with small talk during the holidays. She had become annoyed at the constant questioning of what happened and how are you darling from the Southern women.

Her time spent alone helped the healing. She was tired of people thinking she needed a hug with a shoulder to cry on. It was enough. She would move on when she felt the time was right and no one was going to rush her into another relationship. The horror stories of dating filled the office air enough as it was.

Sarah ascertained the gossip was like living out a best-selling romance novel in real time.

Christmas was coming, dreading the same invitations to attend the traditional office Christmas parties.

Sarah deliberated on the subject over and over. Hearing her inner voice debate with herself as she sat alone in the oversized penthouse she now habited as single woman. Reading a few books on losing a loved one and how to recover helped.

Sarah Joined a support group. Listening to others and talking about her, 'Robert' lifted her spirits, providing temporary comfort.

Attending another weekly group session a younger lady in the group had such a vibrant character while expressing her loss.

At the end of her ten-minute time limit she ended the group with a philosophy of her own that struck Sarah with a different tone than the others.

"The only way to get over a good man was to get under another one."

It was Sarahs AH-HA! moment. That young lady had the perfect idea. It made so much sense to her.

Sarah needed a safer approach to dating. Frolicking in bars at her age was out of the question. Scoring Robert in a private club was a once in a lifetime catch.

Sarah decided to enlist the service of a professional match maker. This approach seemed more plausible. Potential mates should have already completed a vetting process which made more sense. Let them do the work before I get involved in the wrong relationship.

Sarah selected a service. Picked up her cell and made a call to a highly reputable service that catered to business executives. Sarah expressed her requirements for a new partner. She relayed her directions to the agency when and how they were to contact her with potential suitors.

Referring to one of Carley's Southern terminologies she uses all the time. She enlisted professional help to "weed out" the undesirables first. Then hand deliver the high-grade portfolios for consideration.

Speaking with the agency's executive. Sarah was assured her concerns of security, privacy and confidentiality were the priorities of the company.

Sarah agreed to pay the retainer for the finder's fee of fifty percent up front and the remainder only when a match was confirmed. A weekly manilla envelope began arriving via a courier hand delivering it to her in person. A post office box listed as the return address should she forget and leave it somewhere. No one would suspect anything. Each envelope comprised of two to three folders with profiles of men to consider.

Jo-Ann from the agency let Sarah know: a picture of each man will be, clipped to the front of everyone's folder.

New York born Sarah is intrigued at how Southerners name their children with a double first name like, 'Jo-Ann.'

"That's so sweet" is a normal reply to people down here.

The first week passed, then a full month passed as Sarah reads most of the profiles, except for the ones with a not so attractive picture that could be discarded immediately.

Jo-Ann had been waiting for a call from Sarah that had not come. She decided it was time to contact her for feedback.

"Hello Sarah, have you had a chance to view the matches I sent over? "Any interest in meeting with one or all of them?

"I have not" Sarah replied, I cannot decide who would be best just from reading a biography someone wrote about themselves."

"I do agree with you on one point; Jo-Ann, I need to meet these gentlemen personally with a face-to-face meeting. This way I can make a sound decision based on a one-on-one conversation."

"A person can be attractive, athletic, healthy, poor or wealthy, but personality will instantly be judged as soon as they open their mouth."

Jo-Ann suggests Sarah pick five of the best candidates for an all-inclusive one-night, round robin meeting with the best of the bunch, a modified style speed dating meet and greet for cocktails with a one-sided conversation. Sarah was, encouraged to listen to the men while sipping on wine.

"Try to listen and not talk" said Jo-Ann. "You will learn more about a man by Listening" she added.

Sarah could hear her inner voice say.

"Oh Boy this will be challenging to keep my mouth shut for thirty minutes."

Each man had an allotted thirty minutes of time to chat with Sarah. Then she was to take a thirty-minute break to reflect and analyze before the next gentleman arrived.

Jo-Ann gave each man strict rules of engagement to follow. There would be no personnel contact information, to include no business cards were to be offered to Sarah while at the table. The agency would provide feedback to them the next day if Sarah wanted additional information or another meeting. Once your time is up, you are directed to stand up, say goodbye and leave.

Jo-Ann knew her agency could only collect the final fee if Sarah elected to continue with one of them and she needed to control the meeting from start to finish.

If neither of her selections was up to par, nor sparked some interest from Sarah, the agency's contract became null and void..

Sarah entered the restaurant at the prescribed time given to her by Jo-Ann. The kind Matre d' had escorted her to a two-person private table and removed the reserve sign.

With a sweet Southern voice, she heard.

"Your server will be here shortly ma'am."

Wine in hand. Sarah sees her first gentleman coming to meet her. Introducing himself as Giorgos from Greece. No last names allowed; the men must comply with the agency's discretionary policy. Sarah would be, entertained for the first thirty minutes as she listened to this man reveal the secrets of his success as a spice importer. It was all about him with a single question directed at Sarah.

"Do you like to cook? I hope so because I prefer my woman to be home in the kitchen."

Before she could reply. He cut her off to further his position on another subject.

The first thirty-minute break was a needed relief.

The night of meeting more of the same type of arrogant men caused her to lose respect for humanity. The next three strikingly resembled the personality of the previous one that sat down across from her.

An Italian man with a Casanova persona she immediately despised, his breath smelled of a cigar factory. His suit was an original large lapel from the 1960's era to include large white cuffs protruding from the end of his coat.

Sarah could not help herself from thinking.

"He really thinks he is a Casanova."

Up next was a Spaniard with broken English. Clearly unshaven with body odor so bad she wished she had a lit cigar to mask the odor. Sarah sat as far back in her chair as possible, even drawing it away from the table. But it did not help. He spoke about his ex-wife the entire time and how she left him for another woman. It was relentless how he explained how he suspected she was gay all along. He needed to re-marry as quickly as possible to remain in the United States.

Then there was Steven. His portfolio was the most interesting of them all. His intelligence was on her "A" list from reading his profile. Although Sarah concluded that it was written by his mother, once he began to speak. She must have been hoping to get him out of the house and off video games. He was another man obsessed with activities that did not include a significant other.

It was getting late. Sarah was not happy with this match making. Welcome the last thirty-minute break. She was relieved to know there was one half-hour left in what she determined was a disastrous evening attempting to find a new Robert.

Sarah was disgusted as she placed both elbows on the white tablecloth, cradling her face in both hands, she heard Jo-Ann's sweet Southern voice.

"Sarah Honey, are you ok?"

"Why yes Jo-Ann I'm fine."

Jo-Ann proceeded to apologize to Sarah that the last guy on the schedule was no show.

"Now honey you can opt out and go home or I have a client willing to fill in at the last minute. He just happens to be here in the restaurant doing the same thing we set up for you, with our agency. He just finished listening to his selected five women, I think, he is just as disappointed in this process. I pointed you out and he is interested."

"Sarah if you look towards the bar, he is the tall handsome guy ordering a cocktail. His name is Brandon Davies, he owns a seafood packaging company in Charleston, South Carolina.

Sara gazed in the direction of the bar area to see the silhouette of a tall well-built man paying for a round of drinks for himself and another gentleman, not as well dressed standing beside him.

Sarah strained her eyes looking at Brandon as he began turning his head, to look in Sarahs direction, she could see the appearance of manicured facial hair with bold eyebrows.

Jo-Ann could see Sarah locked on the target.

"I will go tell him to come sit with you."

A simple whisper came from Sarah.

"Ok, I can do him, WAIT I MEAN, I can do this, this! I did not mean to say… HIM."

"Calm down Sarah, He's just a guy," said Jo-Ann.

Sarah sits silently as her next match approaches her table. She had already had a conversation with herself in her head.

"One last guy and I am out of here."

"Hello, my name is Brandon Davies, who do I have the pleasure to sit with?"

Sarah slowly extends her hand to greet him. Two hands meet in the middle of the table. Sarah could feel his hand clutching hers with a soft firm assertation of authority. A normal greeting would last seconds then a release with minimal eye contact. Sarah held him in her grip with a long gaze into his eyes as she studied his face.

Brandon now immersed in her beauty as instantly she was with his handsome face. She could feel a surge of energy flowing from his hand to hers as if their souls equally attracted each other. Neither of them wanted to release the others hand.

A brief moment seemed an eternity to both of them as Sarah finally released her grip first and began fidgeting with her napkin then repositioning the silverware on the tablecloth. Sarah was taken back by this man's arrival; he was definitely in control of himself. It was his walk, how he sat, and he had a handsome appearance.

Jo-Ann, who was a short distance away, witnessing the initial session, decided to leave these love birds to themselves and headed out the door without saying goodbye to either client.

Sarah and Brandon went beyond the thirty-minute limit, extending it for a couple of hours. Brandon spoke to great lengths detailing the process of catching shrimp and seafood in the coastal waters of South Carolina. Then how the captains would bring their catch to his processing plant for processing and shipping to retail supermarkets.

Sarah says, playfully. “Well, you must be one of those “BUBBA” shrimp captains?”

“My friends do call me ‘BUBBA.’ It is a Southern thing; you are welcome to call me Bubba if you want to?” replied Brandon.

“Wait, what, they call you Bubba? No way” Sarah chuckled as she responded to Brandon.

“Tell me something Brandon,” Sarah asks.

“What do you need to know.” asked Brandon.

“I need to know what happened in the South after the civil war. Women have double names and men get a quirky short derogative as a surname?” like “BUBBA.”

“I you do not mind Brandon, I will refrain from calling you “Bubba,” It just doesn’t roll of my tongue very well like a Southern borne person and it is not a proper way to address a gentleman.”

“I agree Sarah, it is more for my man friends I have than anyone else.”

Brandon was feeling a little silly, remembering a sitcom from the seventies called Fantasy Island. He changed his voice to impersonate TOTO. "OK then call me Brandon it will be "de plan, de plan." As he pointed to the sky.

The restaurant staff heard the joke and chimed in with laughter in unison with Brandon and Sarah.

Looking around to their amazement, everyone had checked out, leaving them the sole two patrons in the restaurant.

"Well Elvis, looks like we need to leave the building," said Sarah.

Brandon played the part of a southern gentleman all the way to Sarah's S.U.V. as she flicks the unlock button on her key for the lights flash, and a distinctive beep fills the night air. Reaching for the handle she pauses and turns to say goodbye.

Standing beside the closed door, Sarah is a picturesque beauty in the moonlight. Robert is unsure of his next move as he cautiously extends his hand.

Sarah looks down at his hand, without hesitation she looks up at Brandon's face in the moonlight as she commands him.

"DAMMIT, just kiss me."

The sound of leftover New Years fireworks exploded near them at the same time as Brandon took the hint and reached for her waist pulling her in as she simultaneously wrapped her arms around his neck, his lips met hers for the first time.

As with the initial handshake Sarah and Brandon did not want to release the other from the initial captive grip. This embrace was her first since Robert left her. She began to cry.

Brandon stepped back.

"I am truly sorry if I overstepped the boundaries just now?"

Sarah slid her arms down from Brandons shoulders, across his chest down his waist letting her fingers feel his muscular body as she took a step back to admire him.

"The answer to my emotions will have to come another day. For now, it is Good Night."

Sarah let out a big "WHEW, wow that was worth coming here tonight. Take the lead next time soldier or I will schedule you for K.P."

Referring to the military term {Kitchen patrol}

Opening the car door, she made herself comfortable in the driver's seat, pushed the start button, blew a kiss towards Brandon,

Said "good night" again and drove herself back to the penthouse.

Who Is That Guy?

Sarah awakened from a deep sleep from her cell phone vibration. She could feel a hangover setting in and small talk with anyone this early was out of the question. The vibration was relentless. Whoever it was, would not stop calling. Without looking, Sarah reached for the phone, her searching fingers struck it and she sent it tumbling onto the carpet next to the bed.

Sarah needed more sleep after being up most of the night before meetings and greetings. She once again tried to ignore the vibration as long as she could.

Reaching for it again, her mind recalled the memory.

The phone was on the floor. Wanting to leave it there. She assured herself they would call back later or leave a message for listening to it later when she decided to get out of bed.

Sitting up, Sarah pried herself out of bed searching for the phone and stepped on it trying to stand up. Reaching down to retrieve it, she could feel the intensity of the headache surge in her brain. Grasping the phone from underfoot she could see the last three incoming calls were all from Jo-

Ann. Before returning the call, her head started spinning. Nausea was building as her stomach needed to vacate last night's contents quickly.

The porcelain goddess is always there in times of need. Vomiting is not lady like. It quickly reminded her of college parties that always started well but did not end well. A cold reminder of excessive activity that always comes with a declaration of.

"I'm never doing that again."

Standing up to check herself in the mirror.

"This is not your pretty face" said the voice in her head.

A call back to Jo-Ann would have to wait until she had a shower, breakfast to refill the now empty stomach and a cup of coffee. Settling for a quick text to Jo-Ann to have lunch should fend off another volley of calls worked perfectly. Jo-Ann replied with a time of 1:00?

Selecting a restaurant with outdoor seating with close proximity parking for her car. Sarah thought it may be prudent to leave an open bag on the passenger seat just in case her lunch was not received well by her now ruined digestive system.

Jo-Ann found Sarah to be very talkative; Brandon was perfect, in every way she had imagined her next love would be. He was a perfect gentleman and a great kisser, although admitting she was a bit inebriated when it happened, she will give Jo-Ann confirmation of that when she again locks her lips on his in a more appropriate sober setting. Both women agree as they giggle in unison.

Sarah asked.

"I do have one question Jo-Ann, who was the man next to Brandon at the bar last night? Honestly, Jo-Ann, the two men had similar builds and features except his friend did not look as well dressed and had much more facial hair."

"I have no idea." said Jo-Ann.

Sarah thanked Jo-Ann for providing the service and for now her match-making portfolios services would no longer required as she pulled an envelope from her purse with the final payment, sliding it across the table to Jo-Ann.

"I will be in touch in a few months with a full report."

Stood up and headed for her SUV.

The essential element of a newly formed relationship is time spent together. Communication being another key ingredient. The first phase of the process begins.

Once you have passed muster, The first phase of getting to know someone. The next and most crucial step is the emotional connection.

"I like you more than the ice-cream chapter."

Once you begin intimacy, sleepovers, weekend trips. The strength of your bond is now elevated emotionally, and you say the magical three words to each other.

"I love you."

Sarah and Brandon were now committed to a forward relationship of meeting each other more often. Brandon began traveling frequently to stay with Sarah at the penthouse. Likewise, Sarah visited Brandon at his home in Charleston, South Carolina.

Sarah fell in love with the city of Charleston. Being from a big city, she set her goals to learn all she could about Southern culture, so rich with history and of the Civil War.

Brandon knew his town well. Brandon, like Robert, was an excellent tour guide.

Taking Sarah to Historical sites, cultural museums, and an occasional ghost tour.

One Saturday, Brandon and Sarah planned a day of sightseeing near the battery, enjoying the walk along the seawall Sarah noticed a man staring at them as they walked together holding hands.

"Brandon, Sarah asked that man sitting on the bench with the long beard looks familiar. I think I have seen him before."

"You are obviously mistaken; he is a bum that frequents the battery area of Charleston. Let me take you to the market on meeting street, you can find nice artwork there for your penthouse."

"The historical Charleston market was once used to sell slaves as they were offloaded from English ships during the colonial days." Replied Brandon.

"I do not think I have walked in a market like this before. It is very crowded with people," said Sarah.

Sarah turned to ask a vender if she could try on a charming bracelet, which she found interesting. When another person struck her abruptly. She could feel her backside being, groped as a hand had slid from one cheek to the other, Thinking Brandon was being playful at first. Brandishing a big smile, she turned to give Brandon a kiss to show her affection.

The puckered lips were face to face with the street bum she noticed earlier. Startled, he took haste in running away, pushing people out of the way, and disappearing into the packed market.

"BRANDON, there he is again." Sarah yelled.

Brandon had left Sarah's side. Stepping away for a moment of shopping for spices with another vendor on the opposite side of the market. Quickly returning to Sarah asking.

"What happened?"

"Please do not leave me alone again. That street bum with all the facial hair grabbed my butt."

"Oh No! We need to leave the Market it is getting, overcrowded here. Here is an exit. What do you say about grabbing a bite to eat."

"Brandon! "Grabbing" is a bad choice of wording at the moment."

Brandon took Sarah's hand leading the way through the maze of people. Once out in the open streets. Brandon and Sarah walked to Hyman's seafood restaurant.

"This is the best seafood restaurant in Charleston. You are going to love this food. They are one of my best clients."

Sarah and Brandon were finally seated at a private table.

"I could not imagine a better Saturday afternoon than dinning on fried fish and shrimp with you Brandon, what else do have up your sleeve that would top this?"

"I know exactly what we can do to finish our day together." Replied Brandon.

"I bet you do Mr. Romantic."

Stepping out on to the street again Sarah stopped in her tracks. Pointing down the street. With an elevated voice Sarah let Brandon know.

"There he is again."

"I will take care of this; I'm going to have a talk with him."

Leaving Sarah where she stood, Brandon began a military style forced march to catch up with the street bum.

Sarah watched as Brandon grabbed the man by the shoulder spinning him around, then pinning him to the side of the building.

Letting his hand down he began pointing his finger at the man's face.

To Sarahs amazement Brandon abruptly stopped to collect his wallet from his trousers, retrieved some money, and handed it to the bum.

Just as Brandon returns, Sarah sends a volley of questions toward Brandon.

"Who is that guy? Why did you give him money? Where did he go? Do you know him? I thought you were going to punch him. He was, built just like you, tall, muscular, except for the long hair and beard you two looked like twins."

Brandon had to think quickly.

"I do not have a sibling, Sarah. I took care of it, let us go home now and finish what we started with some candlelight."

"I do like how you think Brandon." Said Sarah.

Sarah returned to work on Monday. Summoning Carley into her office, she needed an update on the large life insurance payout she put Carley in charge of a few weeks earlier.

"My discovery returned an answer to who was working on the claim and authorizing the payout to the beneficiary."

"Ok, who authorized the payout?" asked Sarah.

"It seems, your late husband Mr. Killings was the last person reviewing the case with a young intern just before the ….um, crash. I am sorry if this brings up his memory, Sarah. I do hope this information does not make you start crying."

"No Carley I am ok; So, Robert was working on it? Who authorized the beneficiary payout?"

Carley hesitated too long as Sarah broke the hesitation.

"Please tell me who signed off on it, Carley!"

"Where is this intern? "Get him in here now."

"I can't, He quit and has been hired by another insurance agency and no longer works for us, I mean works for you, ma'am."

"Did he authorize the payout," asked Sarah.

"Yes ma'am, I tracked him down to discuss the issue, He assumed Robert gave him the authority to close out the claim, based on his last conversation with Robert, he did what he thought was right in wake of the accident. He was unable to confer with Robert, or an available supervisor since no one had been appointed yet. He made a staff decision on his own. With everything in limbo, he then resigned a week later, figuring he would get, fired soon enough."

Sarah spoke up.

"I know we table these claims for a yearly review for fraud, I would like this one to have a review in six months, let's not let this one get away from us, I will be on vacation with Brandon in Europe for a couple weeks, I am leaving you in charge of the department, I do not want this division to be without a supervisor while I am away."

"Yes ma'am, I will take care of it. Can I use your office?"

"Don't push it, Carley!"

Sarah and Brandon embarked on a European tour of several countries, a pre-bucket list before they reached the age when their joints would be too stiff with arthritis and could not enjoy the trip, or being put on a bus while in a wheelchair did not appeal to them.

Rome, Italy first then off to Paris France. Dining at the Boullion Chartier Grands Boulevard in Paris, Sarah ordered the escargots while Brandon, being a Southern boy, opted for the fresh catch of baked fish with lemon sauce.

"I don't believe I have ever been served a fish dinner with the head still on the fish." said Brandon.

Sarah could only giggle knowing this Southern boy eats everything fried and a baked fish was foreign to him.

The Eiffel Tower was on the list the next day. Standing at the base, looking skyward, Sarah became intrigued by the tower's enormous size. Sarah began thinking to herself.

"What an accomplishment it was to build this as a center piece of this city."

Sarah again realized Brandon had walked away to a leg of the tower. She could see him handing some money to someone standing just behind the leg of the tower just out of her direct line of sight.

Brandon began his return to her. As he closed the distance to her, he could see the puzzled look on her face. Now I am standing face to face with Sarah.

she asked.

"Who is that man? Do you always give money to strangers or bums?"

Without explanation Brndon reached for her hand as he lifted it to his lips, giving her hand a soft kiss, she melted away with thoughts of love, forgetting what she had just witnessed, and he question.

Back at the hotel was the last night of the 2-week tour of Europe. Sarah and Brandon packed clothing into suitcases for the flight back to the states the next day.

Waiting for instructions to board the plane, Sarah opened her laptop to catch up on emails. Brandon was restless and stood pacing in front of Sarah.

"Go get a cocktail Brandon, you need something to calm your nerves, I realize you do not like to fly."

"Great idea, you are right, I do not like flying, I will return before we start boarding."

Brandon stepped up to the airport lounge and ordered himself a bourbon over ice.

"I will have the same," said the man flanking his left side. Brandons posture quickly froze as if he had been, touched, and turned to stone.

Without turning to acknowledge the presence of his unwanted company he asked.

"You are too close; Sarah can see us together."

"Thanks for the drink brother, and thanks for including me on your European trip with Sarah, I am assured she knows nothing of our deal or about me or does she suspect something?"

"Why do you two get first class tickets and I am stuck in coach, I need an upgrade to first class my brother."

"Alright, Danny, since we are on separate flights I will make the change for you, but we need to get you back to being dead and nowhere near me, do I make myself clear?"

"Yes, let's talk mano-e-mano when we get back stateside, this scheme you came up with to fraud the insurance company is not working for me, I am tiring of living in your shadow, I want a life again and a girlfriend like you have now, I am jealous of your situation."

"Listen to me. We have a deal, and that deal is you are DEAD! Now good-bye."

Sarah was deeply concentrating on emails from work.

Brandons voice interrupted her thoughts.

"The plane is boarding, please shut down the computer. I have your bags, let us get on board."

Sarah watched Brandon turn and walk to the check-in counter with their tickets. Under her breath she mumbles. "Yessir, right away sir." From her inner voice she continues her own conversation about Brandon.

"I like this manly authority about him."

Once seated Sarah speaks to Brandon,

"You know what I think about you Brandon?"

"Please say it isn't my butt."

"Oh, geezers please Brandon. I am trying to give you a compliment. You must be the kindest man I have ever known. I witnessed you giving someone money at the tower and just now, just before we boarded, I saw you buy that guy a drink at the airport bar. It must be your Southern hospitality."

Brandon had no response as he leaned over to kiss Sarah on the forehead. Giving her a kiss always puts her in a relaxed mood which causes her to abandon her questioning.

The long oceanic flight gave Brandon time to reflect on the scheme he created to fraud the insurance company. His seafood packing company was in trouble. Foreign seafood was flooding the market driving prices down to levels he had never seen before. His fleet of shrimp boats also needed upgrades and repairs. With his lively hood resting on his company surviving, Brandon had no choice but to conceive the grand plan.

The life insurance policy written for Brandon and his brother Danny was still in place. The policy stated. Upon the death of either sibling, the surviving sibling would become the beneficiary and receive twenty-five million dollars.

That would be sufficient but Brandon, who knew the policy, carried a double indemnity clause.

The policy stated: if either of the insured were to perish due to an accident of no fault. The policy would pay the surviving beneficiary a sum of fifty-million dollars. Basically, double the guaranteed payout of the life insurance policy.

Brandon knew this woman, his Saraha, the beautiful lady next to him. The one person in his life he had fallen in love with. Was the owner of Killings Insurance LLC. The underwriter of his life insurance policy.

Stick With the Plan Dan

It was springtime in the Carolina's, a year prior to meeting Sarah. Brandon made a short phone call to his twin brother Danny.

"Hey brother the spring run of Mahi are migrating North up the gulf stream. Meet me at our boat at the dock in Isle of Palms in thirty minutes."

Danny arrived on schedule. Brandon was already on board the thirty-six-foot contender offshore boat with the three five hundred horsepower Yamaha outboard engines running idle.

"Jump in Danny let us go brother the fish are biting."

Danny removed the mooring lines holding the powerful boat as Brandon selected the waypoint on the plotter chart. The three outboard engines roared as Brandon pushed the throttle arms forward slightly to plain the contender for the short distance down the intercoastal waterway to clear Breach Inlet. On que Brandon was now in the open water of the Atlantic Ocean.

"Hang on brother Danny, I am going to see how many waves we can jump with this beauty of a boat. We should be at the Gulf Stream soon at top speed."

It would be an hour before the Contender arrived at the set coordinates. Brandon rehearsed his plan in his head once again as the bow of the Contender easily sliced through each wave. Its unique design had a 24-degree deadrise bow that drives though the waves allowing the boat to slice into them without jolting its occupants.

Brandon's thoughts were constantly running amuck in his head. The fraud scheme would only work if his brother accepted the plan.

The Chart-plotter sounded the arrival alarm and Brandon drew back on the throttles to slow the boat. They had arrived.

Danny, hearing the alarm and the boat's deceleration, stood up from the captain's bench. Moving quickly, he knew the routine all too well. Get the fishing gear out of the lockers and be ready to fish.

Brandon killed the engines. As he Silently watched his brother search for the tackle that was always on the boat.

"Hey Brandon, where is the fishing gear?"

"Danny my brother, we are not fishing today."

"What are you talking about, why did you bring me all this way out into the Ocean to inform me we were not fishing? You are not making any sense right now."

"Danny, please sit with me. I have something to discuss with you. It is particularly important for us both."

"What are you up to Brandon? What is it now? You always have a plan or a fraud."

"Listen Danny, this may or may not come to a shock to you, but our seafood packaging company is in trouble, big financial trouble."

Danny listened to his brother explain one problem after the other. How the company was struggling to stay operating. How it could not survive without a large influx of cash to clear outstanding loans, cover payroll. He further explained how the fleet of shrimp boats needed upgrades and miscellaneous expenditures.

Danny finally interrupted Brandon.

"If it is cash you need, I have a couple hundred thousand dollars saved for retirement, you are my brother, I can help."

"It isn't enough," replied Brandon.

"How much are we talking about Brandon?"

Brandon hesitated as long as he could. In a choked-up voice he told Danny.

"Several million would be the number."

"If you are asking me for that much cash, you can forget it, I do not have that much Brandon. How did you let this get to this point?"

"Danny my brother, please listen to me. I have a plan so allow me to explain. Just so you know up front. This plan depends on your strict participation. Before I begin, I want to point out we are alone out here. This stays between us, if you decide not to partake in this plan, I will not hold it against you. I will shutter the company and file bankruptcy."

"I don't know about this, but I trust you Brandon, let me hear it first and I will give you, my feedback."

Brandon began the process of how he planned to cash in on the life insurance policy as a beneficiary of the policy that was in effect if either one of them were to perish.

The money would be paid to the surviving brother.

"I can use this money to get the company out of debt."

"Here is the caveat, in the event of an accidental death of either of us. The policy has a double indemnity clause."

"Oh, sweet. How much are we talking about here Brandon?"

"Twenty-five million to the surviving brother and FIFTY MILLION if 'you' die in an accident."

"YOU! As in ME! Just then Danny pointed his finger at himself.

"Why Me?"

"Let us not dive into the if, how and why you Danny. Just trust me, you are the best candidate among us. So let me finish and I will explain the plan."

Brandon continued his explanation with more detail.

To collect on the policy, Danny needed to die in a boating accident. It was elaborate but doable.

Danny could not believe what he was hearing from his brother.

"You are not actually advocating I die so you can get rich, are you?"

"No not in real terms," said Brandon."

"Listen, here is what I am thinking, you take the boat out fishing like you always do because you hardly ever work but, into a storm because you are the die-hard fisherman in the family."

"Because of the storm, a rogue wave swamps the engines, losing power. You begin taking on water, you try to radio for help but then the radio quits in the middle of the transmission and no longer works because of the wave drowning out the electrical systems. You cannot call out Mayday, Mayday or give out your coordinates for a rescue operation."

"I report you missing a couple days later after discovering you did not return to the dock with the boat."

"Wait a minute, how am I supposed to get off the boat as it is going down to Davey Jones locker?"

"I know a very loyal boat captain willing to help. He needs a little cash infusion himself. He is the captain of a grouper fishing boat. He will be in the area to pick you up and safely escort you back to land where you start a new life off the grid. The plan for him to be in the vicinity will not be suspected because his tracking devices are always on, and he is always out fishing for the fish he sells us. I guarantee you, my brother, with the claim money I receive, you will be, taken care of and live better than you do now."

"Sounds like a good plan, Brandon. To recap all this, I take it you are asking me to leave the life I know behind me, change my appearance, my name, virtually, everything I know. Then Danny repeats himself, "Leave my existing life behind?"

"I'm a dead man walking around Charleston, am I correct?"

Danny quickly remembers.

"Wait, we are identical twins. I could walk around, and everyone would think I am you. This is the perfect scenario. It has happened all our lives, we both know this. Your plan might be the best fraud you have ever produced Brandon."

"I just need to know one thing, give me one good reason why I should play along with you and this wild scheme of yours?"

"Actually Danny, I have fifty million reasons."

"HOLY SHITAKI," said Danny.

Danny initially bought into the scheme Brandon laid out for him. Several questions remained to be answered before Danny decided to give his final approval. Being the less intelligent child of the two. Danny planned to back out of the plan. He did not think it had all the pieces in place to be foolproof.

Brandon and Danny decided to work out the plan, step by step, even a rehearsal run of the Contender to the Gulf Stream.

Danny became comfortable as he was convincing himself the plan could work. The next phase they needed to enlist their accomplice.

Captain Charlie was the final piece of their puzzle to make it happen.

One week prior to the fake fishing trip.

Captain Charlie was an older man with grandkids ready to go to college. He decided long ago the life as an angler was something he did not want his grandkids to endure. It was a rough smelly business with little rewards. He instructed each with stern advice to plan on higher education.

Captain Charlie made a commitment to both his grandson and granddaughter that he would find a way to pay for their college tuition. The Granddaughter was already in her first semester as the time had come for the grandson to select a university to attend after his graduation next spring. Both his grandson and granddaughter were, accepted to Clemson and Georgia Southern respectfully. He could not bear the thought of telling them he could not keep the promise he made to pay for their tuition.

Asking the bank was out of the question. His house and fishing trawler were already extended on loans he was struggling to pay for already.

The end of the rope was nearing. No light at the end of his tunnel. Sitting at a local watering hole he expressed his problems as many a drinker does after a few stiff cocktails.

The bartender listening to him whine about his position offered his advice.

“Why do not you go ask Brandon Davies for an advancement on your seasonal catch limit. I am sure he can help you.”

“Craig, you have a great idea son. I might do that tomorrow.”

Brandon had just arrived at his desk to begin the task of pouring over bills that were coming due. Many of them in the pile of paperwork were past due.

Prioritizing the bills in relation to necessity, fuel, phone, electric, water and sewer were a higher priority than small non-essential commodities he could do without if he were to be, cut off for non-payment. Creditors had been calling nonstop, and he figured he could buy some time if he shut the phone off. But how would he take orders and communicate with suppliers, so that plan was shelved quickly.

Brandon's mind was so deep in thought he did not hear captain Charlie entering the building. Charlie had a hard step that anyone would hear this man coming from way off, even if he were walking on a bed of cotton.

The definite knock of a grown fisherman's fist on your office door will get your attention in a hurry.

Looking up to see captain Charlie standing in the doorway half startled Brandon out of his inner thinking

"Hello captain, what can I do you for?"

{That is Southern for, can I help you?}

Captain Charlie was an Irishman whose family tree could be traced back through time in history. He was standing in the doorway to Brandons office as he removed his old, weathered hat, holding it in both hands. His gray thinned hair now being, pushed back with his own hand. No comb needed, there was not enough left to bother owning one.

"Mr. Davies, Can I come in and talk to you for a moment?"

"Sure Captain, have a seat, I was just looking over a few invoices."

Brandon could sense Captain Charlie had something on his mind.

"How are those grandkids? If I remember correctly, captain, they should be ready for college soon I believe. You have been waiting for this day for a long time."

"Yes, yes, I have, and that is why I am here Mr. Davies. I seem to have made a promise to pay for the tuition for both my grandson and granddaughter next fall. You see I have not been a man with fair knowledge of finances over the years since Martha died."

"What are you asking me to do Charlie?"

"Well, I uh. kind of um, need an advancement on my catch quota for next season."

Captain Charlie released his hat with one hand. Raising it in a calming gesture to Brandon.

"Now before you say anything, my boat is seaworthy, not a problem with it. I can guarantee you; I will bring in the fish you need to sell, I have been doing this a long time and have never failed you or your daddy."

Fiddling with his hat Charlie looks down and around the room awaiting Brandons answer.

Brandon was in desperate need of cash himself for his company and here sitting before him was one of his most successful trusted captains asking for help.

It is easy to ask for and receive a fifty-dollar advancement or a quick loan from a friend. But big money is another story. It is the hardest money to acquire. The friend list comes down to no one is available. Banks require you to sign over collateral. Credit cards have limits and if you are aged out or get behind a few payments, you will be shut down. The game is over and the lights to the playing field are now off.

But Brandon was working on a plan, and old Captain Charlie is just the guy he needed to include for it to work out perfectly.

"Captain Charlie. said Brandon. I think we can help each other out. Can you come back tomorrow? I need to make this decision with my brother. Let us say three o'clock PM, here in my office."

"I can be here Mr. Davies. See you then."

Captain Charlie had not been out of the building, exceptionally long when Brandon picked up his phone to dial his brother Danny.

"Hello Danny. Remember our plan? Well, we have the perfect person to help us out. Come to my office tomorrow at two O'clock in the afternoon. I will fill you in on the details before he gets here at three."

"Ok sure thing. But I do remember this is YOUR PLAN! I am still not fully comfortable with all this, but you are my brother, and I trust you. See you tomorrow."

Danny arrives at Brandon's office as planned. Brandon begins the task of filling in more details of his scheme to fraud the insurance company out of millions in life insurance benefits if either twin were to perish in an accidental death.

Danny listened to Brandon describe how it would be a foolproof plan if he could convince Captain Charlie to accept his proposal and get on board.

"Brandon, you are certain Captain Charlie needs money this bad that he would consider this scheme for a minute and not go to the authorities with the evidence and turn on you?"

"Listen to me Danny I do not need to repeat myself again. Charlie is hurting for money; this packaging company needs an influx of cash to survive. Hundreds are at risk of losing their jobs they depend on."

"Ok, ok, you have my word, I will help convince captain Charlie this is in everyone's best interest."

It was three O'clock and Captain Charlie was now sitting in Brandons office. With the door closed and Danny leaning against the window behind his brother, Brandon began laying out his plan. He felt like he was orchestrating a brilliant bank robbery.

Captain Charlie sat in the same chair with a deer in the headlight staring at Brandon while holding his hat in disbelief, He could not believe what Brandon was asking him to do.

A Christian man of faith who believed in hard work and ethics all his life was, now asked to involve himself in a fraud scheme worth, millions.

Brandon finished his pitch as the room fell silent. No one said a word. Brandon leaned back in his office chair waiting for a reply from either his brother or Captain Charlie.

Captain Charlie pondered his response in silence while Brandon and Danny looked dead at him.

Brandon needed to break the stalemate.

"Danny, do you have anything to add to this? Charlie, what are your thoughts?"

Captain Charlie sat in front of Brandon still silent with his head hanging low, deep in thought. His head slowly turning side to side, eyes fixated on the two men in front of him.

Finally, Charlie slowly spoke.

"I am not sure if this is right for me, I do need the money. It will clear up a lot of my debt and provide enough for my grandkid's college tuition. So, if I do accept your offer to participate. What would you be willing to offer me in compensation to keep my mouth shut? I cannot afford to go to prison for this."

"Yea. Danny added; I want to know that number, also Brandon. Just what is our cut to be involved in this? I feel like I am robbing a stagecoach."

Brandon chose his words wisely then replied to both men.

"Let us look at it this way boys. It is a hefty sum of money that will be deposited into a corporate account. Transferring any large amount to each of you quickly will be scrutinized by the bank. Not to mention a red flag that could trigger an investigation by local authorities and the bank will report the transfer to the IRS. I should remind you Danny, you are declared dead. So, I will need to see your last will and testament giving me power of attorney to sell your assets after probate."

Danny abruptly spoke up.

"Whoa cowboy, I did not think long enough on that one."

"It will be necessary Danny to follow through with standard procedures when someone passes. I need to convince everyone you are gone."

Danny was still leaning against the wall behind his brother's office chair.

"You are evading our question, Brandon; I will ask one more time. How much are Captain Charlie and I gaining from this?"

Brandon turned his head to address Danny.

"Go sit next to Charlie so I can look at both of you at the same time please."

Danny dragged another chair next to Captain Charlie and sat down next to him.

"Thank you, now listen to me. As I mentioned earlier, the transfer of money cannot be a direct deposit. Captain Charlie would be legally obligated to pay taxes on the money and as I mentioned the bank would be required to report the transaction to the IRS. And you Danny are supposed to be dead so there is no way I can transfer money to you. So, think about this for a minute. I will be setting each of you up with a credit card to use at your discretion. Keep your spending amounts low first to help with daily expenses and bigger transactions will need to be processed on a discretionary basis so the accounts will not draw attention. This is the best way to resolve all your problems, including mine. It is foolproof, I will take care of you both for a long time. In return you each have a role in this that must be, kept squeaky clean. No one can ever know about this plan."

Captain Charlie sat in his chair with one hand holding his hat while the other hand kept beating on the hat. Brandon sensed he was about to call it off and walk out. Except he was wrong. Captain Charlie rose from his sitting position, extending his right hand to Brandon for a standard handshake declaring he was all in.

Danny followed with the same firm handshake with his brother, then along with Captain Charlie they both stood up to leave.

Brandon was relieved.

"I will be in touch with you both so we can meet again at a different location to work on the details. Now get lost and do not tell anyone we had this conversation."

Did You Get All of That?

A couple of weeks have come and gone by as Brandon finalized details and financial compensation payments. Taking care of Danny's affairs beyond the tragedy was another crucial step he had to take into consideration. A misstep along the way could fold everything into itself.

Brandon was gaining the confidence he needed to implement the plan. It was now time to gather the horses to ride off into the sunset.

Brandon instructed one of his dock hands to purchase a burner type cell phone to use for communication with his brother and Charlie. He figured he needed to use some form of code words to get them together at a place to discuss the details where the meeting would look normal to anyone watching.

With the burner phone in hand. Brandon made a call to Charlie then his brother. He used the same wording to each of them.

"Good afternoon, I would like to have coffee and some breakfast with you tomorrow at eight am, Millers All Day on meeting street is where I prefer to eat."

That was it. He ended each call and threw the phone away in the Bay waters of Charlston, South Carolina.

The next morning, like clockwork, the two associates of crime walked into the restaurant together to meet Brandon who had already ordered and was finishing his last few bites of food.

"The food is excellent here if you two want breakfast."

Neither of the two accepted the offer of food. Responding to the server with "coffee only please."

Coffee in hand and the server out of ear shot. You could hear a pin drop. Both accomplices sat across from Brandon in silence. Neither one started a conversation. Brandon noticed they were so quiet and still he started to chuckle at them.

"Geeze boys, relax guys, don't look so stiff."

Brandon began the conversation.

"Here is how I think this should work. Danny, you pick a day to go fishing offshore, ask a friend to go with you, but make it a workday so they cannot get off work and go with you. You should pick a day with imminent weather warnings in the afternoon for that day to go fishing. It will be a good back-up story that you planned the trip. Get fuel at the dock before leaving so there is a transaction receipt proving you fueled up the Contender."

"Once you are out at the gulf stream. Begin trolling for fish as you would do. Make sure you take the drain plug out of the boat, so it fills with water and sinks in the deepest part of the Gulfstream."

"Since you are an alcoholic, people will think you forgot to put it in if they ever recover the boat at a later date."

That last statement changed Danny's mood.

"Wait, what did you just say about me?

"Let us not argue in the restaurant. We need to maintain our composure here." declared Captain Charlie. "Ok we get Danny's role in all this. What part do I play in this scheme? Please make it clear to me what you need me for in this plan of yours Brandon?"

"Captain, you have the simplest job. You need to have your trawler out at the gulf stream as if you are fishing like you always do. Although you will be waiting for Danny to sink the Contender. You two need to confer the coordinates beforehand where he will be. There is to be no radio contact with each other about this. It may be a clever idea though to talk a little about fishing on the radio so it will sound legit to anyone listening to radio chatter."

"Pluck my brother from his boat as it goes down under the waves in the storm. Ferry him back to shore under the cover of darkness where he can disappear from society. Never to be seen again. I will see to all the problems of your financial affairs as soon as I get the insurance money. Your grandkids tuition will come from an anonymous donor to the college they were, accepted, like a scholarship of sorts."

"Sounds like an easy plan for me. If this is what you are directing me to do. I can accommodate" replied Charlie.

Brandon looked at his brother sitting across from him in the booth.

"Well Danny, what do you say about this?"

"Brother of mine. I say if this is what you have planned for me, I will accept the terms of this plan, you have made it clear. I disappear from society, and you get the insurance money, and I will add, you take care of my estate and future needs. I believe YOU ALONE! have prepared everything."

Brandon had no clue he was in a set up conversation with the two men in front of him. His confession was, now recorded by the F.B.I. Brandon was so proud of himself he voiced the magic words he was, tricked into saying.

"Yes, Danny I alone have come up with this plan, you do not have the capability to figure out how to put it together."

Although Danny wanted to punch his brother for saying that to him. He needed his brother to openly admit this was his plan alone.

The meeting ended after that statement from Brandon as they paid their bill. Exited to the street, stopping for one last handshake with each other.

With the surveillance van parked a few hundred yards down the street. Brandon was so full of himself he never noticed the fake telephone company name printed on the side doors.

Captain Charlie said.

"I need a drink, Danny how about you and I find a quiet place to have a Bloody Mary?"

"Fantastic idea Charlie. I need a stiff one at this moment."

Brandon turned away from them both and walked away, never looking back to see if they had left the area. Once they confirmed Brandon was around the corner and out of sight.

Danny said aloud.

"Did you get all that?"

Captain Charlie followed suit.

"I hope they did."

The two turned left and walked down the street to the awaiting van parked near the restaurant. As they approached the sliding door came open. Two F.B.I. agents in full uniform stepped out of the van.

"Great job guys. Let us get those wires off you and get you on your way, Mr. Charlie you did mention something about needing a Bloody Mary, right?"

Danny and Charlie stood at attention while the agent disconnected the microphone from their shirts. Danny was standing at the perfect angle to peak in the van. He could see a monitor with images of them sitting in the booth with his brother. They obviously had contacted the owners of the restaurant to tap into the video surveillance cameras ahead of their visit with his brother.

A sick feeling began turning his stomach. Danny's inner voice began questioning himself.

"What was he thinking? Turning into an informant against his own Brother."

The Irishman's voice broke Danny's thinking.

"Come on Danny, let's go to the Blind Tiger for a couple Bloody Mary's."

Danny accompanied Captain Charlie on a slow walk to the Blind Tiger. Neither exchanged conversation during the walk.

Arriving at the bar they could see two empty bar stools recently vacated. Quickly commandeering the seats before the crowd realized the absence of a couple with warm butts propped on them had vacated them moments earlier. The two men begin drinking Bloody Mary's just like everyone else in the morning in Charleston South Carolina.

Finally, after the second drink was finished, Captain Charlie was feeling his normal talkative self and began to strike up a conversation with Danny. Albeit under his breath at first, he said,

"What are we doing?"

“WE? Danny asks, “are not discussing this in public, so shut up and enjoy your liquid breakfast, I will get the tab and talk to you later.”

Danny exited the Blind Tiger into the bright South Carolina sunshine. Quickly reaching for his sunglasses to shield his dilated pupils from the sun’s rays.

Bars are dimly lit facilities for a reason. Alcohol consumption opens the pupils of your eyes which naturally filter the bright sunshine as you walk outside. This is why it is, called the Blind Tiger effect, and the indicator officers of the law use while interrogating you at a traffic stop when they suspect you have been drinking.

Danny went for a long walk to figure out his demise. The streets of Charleston were busy with couples on vacation. One couple stopped him to ask directions to the old Market. Explaining directions with the best route to take. The man reached out to shake Dannys hand in gratitude.

As he did his sport jacket opened to reveal a service style Storm Ruger 9 MM attached to his belt. A glimmer of badge clearly attached to the pistol holder.

Danny brushed it off at first thought as he realized he was being followed. The couple asking for directions must have been part of the surveillance team.

Danny once again felt sick to his stomach. The plan and the decision to involve the local authorities in Brandon's plan were in place. There was no turning back at this point.

The public safety investigators had informed Danny that no crime had been committed yet. If this all goes as they had planned, then the F.B.I. would have greater involvement. If he cooperated with them in the investigation. No charges would be filed against him or Captain Charlie.

Back at the Blind Tiger. Captain Charlie was served a few more drinks by another agent posing as the bartender.

A young agent straight out of the F.B.I.'s academy was, tasked with getting Captain Charlie intoxicated enough he would start talking freely and concur the full scope of the plan. Two telling the same story in separate locations at separate times could give them enough to commit to a full investigation of the crime.

The F.B.I.'s plan was successful. Charlie was a treasure of information. Every detail of Brandons plan came spilling out with a few extra Bloody Mary's.

Captain Charle was, helped into a cab by a couple of employees and taken back to his house to sleep off the alcohol.

The young agent phoned his supervisor to update what he had been told. Even under intoxication. The story remained the same. The plan was now confirmed to be all Brandon's.

Captain Charlie never suspected he had been, interrogated by an agent of the F.B.I. while drinking his Bloody Mary's.

One Month Prior

Danny had taken the first step to contact local authorities. Nervously he told them his story. After a lengthy interview. The Charleston police directed Danny to the satellite field office of the F.B.I. This was beyond their scope and the money involved with the fraud scheme was more than they figured possible for them to manage without the help of the federal authorities.

"Good morning, Mr. Danny Davies, Is this your real name sir? And do I have your permission to record our conversation today?"

"Yes, it is. and yes, you have my permission to record."

"Thank you for coming in to see me. I am special agent Clarence Downing of the F.B.I insurance fraud investigation unit. I have been, informed by the Charleston public safety you have some interesting information regarding a potential insurance fraud that might be occurring."

"There is no MIGHT BE sir, it is in the works."

Agent Clarence downing was a tall African American man wearing a tailored three-piece suit that gave him a distinguishing look. He spoke with a commanding voice. He was not a man to mess with. a thirty-year veteran of service with the F.B.I. he had a sixth sense to know when he was, being, played by an informant.

"Alright Mr. Davies can you state your full name for the recorder and the nature of your visit today?"

"Sorry I am a little nervous being here."

"We understand this is a big step for most people in your position. So, Mr. Davies let us get, started with your statement and we can assess if the bureau needs to get involved in a crime local public safety should be managing in the first place."

"Here let me adjust the microphone closer to you so you will be more comfortable. Again, begin with your name and the reason for the visit today."

"Danny took a breath and calmly began the task of relaying the information into the microphone and to agent Downing who had a pad of paper for taking notes to refer to if he needed additional questions answered before they would finish for the day.

"Let me get this straight."

Referring to the note he scribbled on his pad.

"You stated there is another person involved in the perpetration of this crime? A Captain Charlie, you claim works for your brother?"

"He does not actually work for my brother. Captain Charlie is a trawler, Captain. He is an independent angler providing a catch limit to the processing facility. He needs cash in a bad way. So, Brandon included him in on the scheme."

"I see, how do I get in touch with him?"

"I mentioned to him this is not a good thing my brother has been planning. Neither of us want to go to prison for participating in an insurance fraud of this magnitude."

Agent Downing did not like the sound of Danny's statement and asked.

"Are you saying if it was a smaller amount, you might be ok with the plan and willing to perform what he has asked you to do, without notifying the authorities?"

That statement from agent Downing shocked Danny to his core as he looked up at agent Downing's glaring eyes. Now his inner thoughts raged inside his head as he spoke.

"Am I going to prison for ratting on my brother? What am I going to do now? He has me right where he wants me."

Agent Downing began to speak, breaking Danny's concentration.

"Let me assure you Mr. Davies, at this point you have not committed a crime. You are not being detained; You came here on your own to provide details of a pending crime. Your help and cooperation will be appreciated. We would like to have Captain Charlie come in and give us his version in his own words. Again, we need to contact this, Captain Charlie. The bureau will finalize a course of action after we receive his statement and fully review the evidence presented by both of you. Can you convince him to come in to speak with me? At this point it is in his best interest to cooperate."

Danny was uneasy about making the recording, and concluded it was in his best interest.

"Yes of course, I understand. I am meeting him for cocktails again this evening. He is more cautious than I am. His wife has passed away and he has grandchildren to think about."

"If you don't mind, I have a few more questions before you leave the room Mr. Danny Davies."

"Are you a drug addict?"

"Any issues with alcohol?"

"Any financial action you may be involved in?"

"Do you have a problem with your brother that would cause you to make up a story to get him in trouble?

This last barrage of questions tore into Danny hard. Responding with a stern voice.

"I can assure you Mr. special agent Downing, I am neither of that. I came here in good faith, and I demand the respect for my actions today are we, are finished talking."

"I will assure you Mr. Davies, you now have my respect. Now please convince your Captain Charlie friend to come and talk to me. The agent outside is waiting to escort you out of the building, GOOD DAY SIR."

Danny exited the office and immediately called Captain Charlie.

"I did it, I had the meeting with the F.B.I. are you ready to have a couple drinks and I can discuss your position in taking down my brother. He needs to be the one to go to jail, not us."

"Meet me at Montreux Bar & Grill in Summerville in an hour." Replied Captain Charlie

"On my way Captain."

Placing his cell phone in his back pocket. Danny found his SUV adorning a parking citation stuffed under his windshield.

"Just my luck." He grumbled aloud as he retrieved it from the windshield.

Driving to Summerville, SC is no easy task. The traffic is as bad as it gets with development outpacing the highway upgrades. Two lanes need to be four or six in some places.

The slow driving of aging Southern demographics did not help. Danny was anxious to get to Captain Charlie as quickly as possible.

Nearing an overpass he had plans to exit the side road and make a quicker drive on interstate 26. Taking one look out the side window he realized the interstate was at a standstill. Assuming from a wreck farther up the road. In his haste to make his decision to stay on course with the side road. A big yellow school bus exiting the interstate off ramp seized the opportunity of the opening in traffic Danny provided in his hesitation.

"Unbelievable, I cannot believe I am behind a school bus full of Girl Scouts returning from a field trip."

A short distance away the bus turned into a church parking lot and Danny was, back again up to speed heading to his rendezvous with Charlie.

Finding an open spot to park, Danny makes his way to the entrance. Once inside he finds his friend two cocktails deep ahead of him.

"Sit down and order a double to catch up. So, you met the feds did you now?"

"Yes, Charlie, as a matter of fact I did."

"Are you happy with the outcome? Are we in trouble? "If I need to turn myself in, it will be after I have had a few more of these."

Charlie raises his rocks glass in a solute to Danny.

Danny looked at the bartender and ordered a double Crown Royal on the rocks.

"I got assurance we are not in any trouble. At this point, he said no crime has been committed. But it is in our interest to cooperate now that they have been, made aware of the plan.

Hopefully, Brandon is committed to follow through with it."

"Alright, I guess it is my turn to be a squealer."

"Charlie, I know it is alcohol talking, so, I ask you this. Are you willing to go to prison for my brother? Would your daughter and grandkids be ok with knowing you played a part in a multimillion-dollar fraud scheme?"

"Do not be so stupid Danny, of course not. I was not comfortable with it in the first place. I was going along with it because you were there in the office. I thought both of you were doing the planning."

"Ok Charlie let us get one thing straight between us. I am not the one who produced this plan. So, put that to bed and leave it there."

Danny was furious at Captain Charlie's alcoholic outburst directed at him. He found it difficult to accept the mere accusation he had anything to do with planning this scheme.

Danny motioned for the bartender to bring his tab. He was again ready to leave his friend sitting at the bar drowning himself in Bloody Mary's. Signing his name on the credit card receipt, Danny opened the contacts of his phone to agent Downing's number. Using the same pen to write the agent's cell number on a bar napkin.

"Here you cranky old geezer. Give this guy a call, ASAP."

Danny decided it was time to leave everything alone for now and drove himself to the docks to board his thirty-six-foot contender named.

'Seven-Out.'

Danny needed to get away and took the contender out for a ride. He needed to find the perfect place to sink the boat.

A contender boat is a magnificent machine designed to travel to the roughest salt waters from any coastline. Enabling the owner of these vessels to fish when they wanted to fish and not dependent on weather or wave conditions. Its sleek frontal deadrise allows the vessel to cut through waves like butter with minimal jolting to whoever was captaining.

Engineered to be comfortable while operating at high speeds that no other vessel its size could maintain. The design is for serious tournament anglers wanting to arrive at a coordinate and return just as fast, thus maximizing time for lines in the water.

Danny's mind is no different than any other human. Once he arrived at his favorite coordinates, some sixty-five miles offshore of Charleston, South Carolina, the Gulf

Stream begins to drop off into three-thousand feet of water of the North Atlantic Ocean. Deep enough to sink a boat where no one would take the effort to retrieve it.

Slowing the boat to idle, his mind begins to initiate thoughts. A process we all begin when we are alone or need to work out some details of our life.

"I need to make this convincing to my brother. This deep water will be the perfect spot to sink Seven-Out."

If I tell him where I plan to sink this boat. If I present a foolproof plan to him, he will have confidence in my execution of the plan to follow through with every detail. Without a convincing strategy of my own, this could all go south on me. I do not want to look like a liar to agent Downing."

The next morning.

The morning showers were pummeling the metal roof over Captain Charlie's head as he lay in bed cursing another hangover.

Like every alcoholic, the next morning is a brutal reminder of the previous day's habit. His mind says the same thing it has heard a hundred times before.

"I have got to quit this drinking."

Rising from his sweat-soaked sheets, he stumbles into his restroom to empty the swollen bladder that was so painfully full. It was the reason he woke up in the first place.

Back at the bedside he grabs a menthol cigarette from his nightstand. The first puff of the day in his lungs he looks down at a folded napkin that was placed beneath his pack of smoke.

With a cigarette dangling from his lips as smoke dribbles upward across one eye making it squint. He could not recall what the napkin was there for or why it was there. His first thought conjured up old times of getting a maiden's name and number while drinking the night before at the bar.

He reaches for the napkin and unfolds it.

"Well let's see what I got myself hooked up with. This is definitely not what I expected to see."

There was a name and a number for the special gent Clarence Downing. With a message written by Danny.

Call him ASAP.

Agent Clarence Downing was about to leave his office with another agent for lunch when his cell phone rang out.

“Hello this is agent Clarence Downing, with the Charleston division F.B.I, how may I help you?

Calrence Downing listened to what, appeared to be, an older man with a deep scratchy voice attempting to mutter out a sentence. The man on the phone spoke an Irish accent mixed with low-country Geechee, drawl. It was hard for the agent Downing to understand as he stood slightly bent at the waist pressing the phone hard into his ear to drown out the noise of the office atmosphere.

“Who is this? Agent Downing asked, “Do you know you have called an agent of the F.B.I. sir?”

Clarence quicky raised his head looking up at the ceiling.

“Mr. Charlie! I mean, Captain Charlie, Good to hear from you. Yes, I can meet you this afternoon. Is three O’clock ok with you sir? Good, I will see you then.”

Clarence Downing ended the connection with Charlie. Looking over at the agent ready to accompany him to lunch. Agent Downing broke into a smile.

“We have a hot one, the old Captain is coming in this afternoon. If this goes down, it will make national news when it is all said and done. Let us get some lunch and I will fill you in."

Agent Downing finished preparing his questions for Captain Charlie when his receptionist stepped into his office.

"I have a MR., well a Captain Charlie here to see you, he says he has a three o'clock. I put him in the interrogation room already for you."

"Thank you, Christine, I will be right there."

Clarence Downing opens the door to the only interrogation room. Sitting slumped in a chair wreaking of dead fish and cigarette smoke is a short stout gray haired man holding a ball cap with both hands. Clarence extends his arm in greeting as he feels the grip of a strong weathered hand.

"Mr. Charlie, how are you today sir?"

"It is Captain Charlie to you if you do not mind. Everyone calls me Captain Charlie."

"Ok Captain Charlie it is. Can you tell me in your own words why you are here? And do you agree with being recorded?"

A grumbling voice responds from the other side of the table.

"I suppose recording this is necessary for you folks. I do not talk a lot. I am a good angler. A darn good angler. I got a good family. Do not need nothing happening to me or them."

"Yes sir, I understand your position. Can you give us specifics about a plan Mr. Brandon Davies has to fraud his insurance company out of several million dollars?"

"I do not know much about no swindling any insurance company. All I was supposed to do was be at the gulf stream to pick up his brother Danny when he sank his boat and take him back to the hill. If I do this, I get my grandkids tuition paid for helping his ass do this, that is all he asked me to do, that is all I know, that is all I want to know, nothing else."

"Mr. Excuse me, Captain Charlie, are you willing to wear a wire to help us get the details for a conviction?"

"I figured you boys would ask me to do something stupid like that, before I agree to help you, I need to know, am I going to jail for my participation?"

"No sir, you have not committed a crime at this point. One thing I must point out is that I can't tell you. If you decide not to participate or Brandon Davies does not follow through with his plan. We do not have a case against anyone. No crime, no arrest, no time."

"Ok then, I do not like it, but I need to help somehow. I never liked that sneaky brat anyway; his father was a better man than he ever was."

Captain Charlie spent the next hour and a have detailing his involvement on Brandons plan.

Agent Downing finished asking questions and was now convinced Captain Charlie was legitimately telling the truth.

"I think we have enough for now Captain. Thank you for coming today. We will be in touch with you soon. One final thing. It will be in your best interest not to say anything more about this to anyone, especially Brandon Davies."

Captain Charlie left the building as discreetly as he could. Looking up and down the street for any sign of an agent following him to his truck. Or better, yet he was nervous Brandon would have followed him to prove his loyalty.

One thing agent Downing was sure of in his line of work. There are very few truly intelligent criminals in the world. They all get caught, in some way, at some point.

Not Enough Evidence

Danny and Captain Charlie were meeting with the F.B.I. on a regular basis. Nothing had been initiated by the bureau to stop Brandon or arrest him on suspicion of committing fraud. It was a lesser charge and Clarence Downing needed a bigger case to make the headline news.

Danny accused him of stonewalling. But Clarence had a plan of his own. His idea was to pressure his informants to implement the plan in full. He wanted the attention of a full-blown press conference with all the media presents. He needed a promotion out of South Carolina, and this was his ticket to stardom.

Holding back on arresting Brandon made perfect sense. Let these good ole Southern boys steam a little in their own sultry heat of Charleston, South Carolina. When the time was right, the dirty laundry was, now aired out. He would be a hero to the bureau.

Danny met with agent Downing repeatedly to provide information and to get a feel for when he should begin to sail out into the ocean.

"Agent Downing. There is a storm coming which will be the perfect time to make this happen. I will tell my brother tomorrow is the day I will be leaving the dock to sink Seven-Out and disappear from society. When will you arrest him then?"

"Danny neither of you have committed a significant crime with enough evidence to get a decent conviction for a criminal offense. Once he makes the claim to the insurance company for the benefits then we have enough to start the legal process with a warrant from a judge until then, we have insufficient cause to arrest him beforehand. Now, if we intervene with an arrest for conspiracy to commit a crime, he will be out on the streets back at work in less than 24 hours. I am positive you and Captain Charlie do not realize the repercussions this will mean to you both?"

"So, you are telling me, I have to make good on everything that my brother has planned, including sinking a half million-dollar boat in the Atlantic Ocean, in three-thousand-feet of water?'

"I know it sounds crazy to you. Please understand our position when it comes to having enough evidence for the bureau to make a case in convicting a criminal of this magnitude. The other aspect, I am trying to beat into your head is, he needs to be, put away for good, or your life and Captain Charlie may be subject to dangerous repercussions from your brother over time."

"Entender Amigo?"

"This is taking way to long agent Downing. WAY, WAY, too long."

"Listen to me Danny, you need to be patient with us. One major issue is that your brother needs to secure the money from the insurance company and begin distributing it. That action alone will put him away for a long time."

"Once a conviction is, secured and sentencing is set it will be an enjoyable time for you and Captain Charlie to get away from Charleston and start a new life. After you two testify of course. Adding Captain Charlie can use the money to pay for his grandkid's tuition."

"What about any money he gives me?" asked Danny.

"We are not concerned about retrieving money for insurance companies. That is up to them and the civil court to retrieve any losses on their part. We deal with the criminal aspect only."

"Danny, it is well worth noting, he must commit a crime. Talking is not enough evidence to arrest someone or secure a conviction. By the way, if I may suggest an alternative to your plan for sinking that beautiful vessel."

"What would that be?" asked Danny.

"You really do not have to sink it at all. Your brother will never know if you did or did not, now, will he?"

Danny sat in the chair in front of agent Downing's desk and stared into his eyes with disbelief he did not think of this himself.

"Agent Downing, you have just confirmed what Brandons said to me when he was pitching the scheme. I am not smart enough to think of a good plan."

“I get it now. I have your word on this, neither me nor Captain Charlie will be, arrested for playing along with Brandons scheme if we cooperate with the F.B.I.?”

“Correct, you have my word as an agent of the F.B.I. Look Danny, the bureau checked you both out thoroughly, neither of you have any priors. Pretty clean records from what we found out, asides from a couple parking violations, which this city hands out like candy at a Halloween party.”

“Somehow, I think I may need that in writing from you as a guarantee of safe passage in the future, Agent Downing.”

“Alright Danny Davies we are now, finished for today. By the way, in case you have not noticed we have all three of you under surveillance 24/7.”

“Oh! trust me I already know that.” Said Danny.

Cursing the downpour of a summers afternoon rain shower that always continues through the evening hours on the coastline of South Carolina, Danny steps out of the glass doors of the Charleston field office without an umbrella, using quick strides to reach his car.

Danny decides to meet Captain Charlie one last time at Montreux to give him another update from Agent Downing.

"Just what did Five-O say now?" as Charlie ordered his evening bourbon. I am sure it was a crock of lies, was his mouth moving? If it was, we know he was lying."

"Charlie, I completely understand your frustration, given the circumstances. But here is your lucky charm. We must convince Brandon we are ready to follow the plan. For the F.B.I. to get enough evidence for a conviction, we have to complete our part of this plan. Then and only then can Brandon initiate the start of the claim process for payment of the loss of life benefits from the insurance company. Once he gets his hands, on the money the fraud is completed. He will begin transferring to us what he promised and here is the good part."

"What! there is a good part? Replied Charlie.

"Yes, said Danny, Listen to this. The F.B.I. does not give a rat's ass about recovering the money for the Insurance company. They do not deal with corporate losses or their problems. It is up to the insurance company to recover it. If they even decide to do so. If we get enough money from

Brandon, including the money he pays to a college for tuition. It is a deal done; we have it, and they may never come looking for it. If they get a conviction on Brandon."

Captain Charlie turned his head to look at Danny, seated next to him at the bar.

"I take back what I said about you before. You are just as brilliant of a sneaky rat as your brother, just a little more, slick about it."

"Thanks Captain I needed to hear that. So, lets toast to getting this, show on the road."

"One more thing we need to agree on Captain."

"What now slicky dickie?"

"You are so much fun to play with Captain Charlie. Let us agree from this point on, 'NOT' to talk to that special agent anymore. If he is true to his words, we should be finished with him forever. He can find out this went down from the nightly news on a local channel."

"I will toast to that, Danny."

"I have more to divulge about our part in the game."

"Dammit, I knew all this was too good to be true. What else are you going to do Danny?"

Danny was taken back with Captain Charlie's tone. He grabbed his cocktail and finished it off in one long gulp. Slammed it down on the bar and grabbed Captain Charlie with the shirt sleeve to get his attention.

"Listen to me you old geezer, I do have some smarts about me. I may be my dysfunctional brother's twin, but I do not care much for looking exactly like him all the time. Do not let my long hair and unshaven face give you thought to believe I do not have any brains. I am not as dumb as I might look."

"OK, calm down man, let go of my shirt sleeve. Tell me what you are thinking, before the bouncer comes over here and beats you up.

"You know how to get under my skin Captain."

"My apologies. Danny, now spill, the beans will you."

Danny calmed himself down and ordered another cocktail before continuing his conversation.

"I do not see why I need to actually sink the boat."

"What are you proposing then?" asked Captain Charlie.

"Listen I will meet you at your favorite grouper fishing spot about forty miles out. It is shallow enough that I can set an anchor. The boat will be fine for a couple of days. Then I will need you to take me back to the boat and I will take it somewhere."

"I take back what I said previously. You are as dumb as you look." Said Captain Charlie.

"Why do you say that?" Announced Danny.

"In the first place. Your brilliant plan has one big flaw. The Coast guard will be combing the Ocean for your body with their Helo for at least a week. If they find the boat moored out there floating with no one on board and trust me, they will find it. This whole plan goes South the instant they find the boat, floating at anchor. You know your brother will save his skin by pinning this scheme on you and me, I bet you did not think of that twist in the details of your plan, did you?"

"You are correct. Ok then, we will sink the boat. I really hate that part of the plan."

"I refer back to my last statement about you not being the brightest bulb on the tree." Said Captain Charlie.

Adding insult to injury.

"Your momma must have dropped you on your head when you were a baby. Do you have anything else to add before we leave the bar?"

Danny finished his cocktail and replied.

"I have nothing further to say."

Then added as he mumbled under his breath.

"Wasn't my plan anyway."

"Good, now let us go tell your brother we are set to go, we have a boat to sink."

No Plan Is Perfect.

Sarah fell deeply in love with her new Southern man. He was a perfect gentleman that everyone liked, except for Carley,

Carley knew everything about Brandon.

Carley's time investigating the mysterious disappearance of Danny Davies uncovered a fact no one else knew. Danny Davies had a twin brother named Brandon.

While investigating the large beneficiary payout Carley discovered a connection between the payee and Sarah's beau "Brandon" may be one in the same.

As an investigator it was her job to suspect fraud first and prove innocent afterwards. The details did not add up to the claim of Danny drowning on a fishing trip in a storm. He was an accomplished boat captain with years of experience. Why did he not have an E.P.I.R.B distress beacon? Why was there no life raft on that vessel? It was surely big enough to require one. He was an accomplished boater. Why did a half million-dollar boat sink in the first place? Too many questions unanswered as the evidence failed to line up.

No boat was ever found, nor had a body ever recovered. It was the same answer every time it was, brought up to search and rescue. "Probably eaten by sharks that far out in the ocean," was their reply every time.

Carley left the case open until it was time to tell Sarah, and she did not want to be the one to break the bad, news to her new boss.

The weekend approached.

It was Brandon's turn to come to Columbia to visit Sarah for the weekend. The two mutually agreed on taking turns visiting each other so neither would get burned out going one way all the time. They enjoyed being with each other so much it was a routine of dinner and back home for a cocktail or an all-night fling in bed.

Brandon was comforting to make love with, but he was not her Robert. He filled a void she needed. Justifying it all by adding no one is perfect at everything. She accepted his inability to make her climax like Robert. It was something she decided to live with.

Danny was supposed to play Dead. Stay away from Brandon at all costs, including anyone he had ever known in his life.

A celebration of life sealed the deal, and life went on as usual for Brandon.

Sitting in his office in Charleston late one evening he heard someone enter the building through the back door, footsteps on the old wooden floor were getting closer to his office. Brandon looked up from his paperwork to see his brother standing at the office door.

"Hello brother,"

"What are you doing here Danny? I see you have shaved and cleaned up.

"I have been thinking about this arrangement we have, and I think we need to re-negotiate the terms."

"We have a plan, Danny, please do not screw it up."

"I tried to stay hidden, stay away, live a quiet life. It is not working for me Brandon. You have a girlfriend, I do not! You have a perfect life, I do not."

"You cannot be serious? What do you want me to do at this point Danny?"

"I will go back to being a dead man under one condition."

"What is it? Is it more money? I have already given you and Captain Charlie quite a lot of money."

"This is not about money, Brandon."

"Then what is it? Make it quick before someone sees you in here."

"I want to have your life for one night, well maybe one weekend, then I promise to disappear again."

"This is bull crap Danny; you cannot be me."

"I can and I will. We are identical twins if I need to remind you. I get what I want, or this charade is over with. I cleaned up and I can walk out of here right now and play with you, all dressed up like you, No one will suspect I am not you anywhere I go tonight. You captivated me on that boat, I had to listen to you, and I agreed to play along to help you, so this company survived. It is you, my brother who will listen now."

Brandon, rose from his comfortable office chair to look at Danny man to man, while he struggled to maintain his emotions. He desperately wanted to hurt his brother.

"Alright you win, what is it you want? Danny"

“Before you flip out, just listen, I want a weekend with Sarah.”

“You are absolutely nuts if you believe I will play along with that.” Snarled Brandon.

“I know everything about you and her. Where she lives, the company she inherited. The one you frauded out of fifty million dollars. Listen to me Brandon, we are identical twins in every anatomical way. Except I am, left hand, and you are right hand dominant, that is our only known difference we know between us. Other than that little detail there is no difference in us that anyone has ever been able to notice. We have been, mistaken for each other all our lives.”

“You are out of your dam mind Danny if you think I will agree to this ridiculous plan.”

“Remember your loyal grouper fishing friend, Captain Charlie? The one you quit paying hush money too. He is a little pissed and might just contact the F.B.I. with his version of evidence against you. I have him convinced to hold off, if you agree to keep paying him and you agree to my terms.”

“You two have descended into black mailing me?”

“I guess you can put it that way Brandon.”

Brandon could not believe what he had just heard from his brother. While growing up, it was fun to switch places. A trick they played on everyone who knew them from childhood. Brandon, being a bit more intelligent than Danny, would take exams for his brother in college to help him get his degree. Now this was different. It involved his sweet love Sarah. Brandon was not prepared to go this far with his brother. It was a pact they made in high school to never cross this line.

Brandon went deep inside himself to search for an answer. If he agreed to this, the company survives, and life goes back to normal. Refusing Danny's request and his entire world topics include his relationship with Sarah. The thought of being jailed for fraud carried a heavy price he could not accept.

"Look Danny, I can offer you a million dollars to not go through with this request."

"Money will not help Brother. Remember what you said, you cannot transfer large sums of money? It is beyond the money at this point."

"Ok Danny one weekend, one weekend, no more. Then you keep playing dead, you swear to me you will disappear and never come back again?"

"I promise brother. Sarah is coming here this weekend, correct?

"How do you know that? Where are you getting information about me and Sarah?

"I cannot tell you how I know Brandon. Trust me I know."

Danny wanted to blurt out the answer. Agent Downing had been feeding him information about his brother's location for weeks now.

"Never mind! said Brandon. I am impressed you have the intellect to find out details of my relationship with Sarah."

"Sarah will never know it is not you Brandon, this will be fun, by the way I will need your house and car keys. I plan on being the one to meet her at the door this weekend."

Brandon reaches deep into the front pocket of his pants, grabs his keys, and tosses them to Danny.

"I fail to see the fun in this for me."

Danny, A.K.A. Brandon sets up residence awaiting Sarahs arrival. Driving from Columbia Sarah was feeling frisky as the road vibration coupled with thoughts of being with Brandon again excited her to no end. She anticipated a quickie to first settle her desires then they will go out to dinner.

Sarah pulled in Brandons driveway in Charleston with eager anticipation to jump into Brandons arms. Planning to surprise Brandon by grabbing his hand in one swift motion while leading him to the bedroom, then finishing the weekend with other activities after she was satisfied.

"Everyone has a plan that no one else knows about."

Sarah was determined to initiate intimacy with the man she thought was Brandon, a typical laid back gentle shy man when it came to sex. Her plan was to take the lead tonight.

Little did she know, the Sloth was substituted for a Serengeti lion isolated from his harem for too long.

Danny was waiting inside for Sarah as she entered the house. Standing in the living room with his shirt unbuttoned, Sarah could see his muscular chest and toned six pack abs.

Overwhelmed with emotion. Her plan went into execution quickly. She reached for her hero's hand to lead the way.

Danny sensed his opportunity was upon him. Instead of Sarah leading the way he held her hand with a stronger grip. Just strong enough to pull her back into him. He could smell the fragrance of her sweet perfume. Her hair was soft as he used his left hand to gently let her hair slide between his fingers. Grabbing her hair with a loving grip he tilted her head backwards. Meeting her lips with a playful touch of his tongue to her lips. Sarah has never experienced the soft slow kisses from Brandon as she begins to enjoy the moment. Her thoughts are of Brandon; He has never been so romantic as his left hand is beginning to explore her body. First her breast as he gently squeezes her nipples. Sarah cannot help but feel relieved she did not wear a bra on this trip. The sensation of her man's touch was releasing a small orgasmic feeling in her body.

His left hand slid down to her thighs as he caressed her bottom. A full hand full as he squeezes her cheek, pulling her close to his hips as possible. Sarah was at a height she had never experienced with Brandon. His left hand released its grip on her backside, moving to the front his fingers lifting her sundress.

Sarah's mind began to speak to her.

"Glad I planned on going commando."

The left hand found a warm wet reception. Sarah began to moan aloud as his fingers probed around and around creating a river of love juice flowing down her legs. Sarah was convinced she was in heaven and did not want to leave.

It was with one quick motion Brandon AKA Danny reached down with both arms swiftly lifting Sarahs legs to wrap around his waist as he marched the two of them into the bedroom.

Sarah began unbuckling her man's belt, releasing it.

His muscular arms embracing her as he was tossing her on the bed, he finished removing his pants as Sarah was ready to receive him. Pulling her toward the end of the bed and using the footboard to anchor his feet he began thrusting into Sarah.

Sarah was finally able to relax as her lover rolled away lying beside her.

she asked.

"Do you need a hot towel to clean off my darling?"

"Thank you for offering, I am ok for now. You are amazing Sarah, I never expected it to be this good."

"What does that mean Brandon? we have been making love for a while now.... Dear. Albeit not as intense but we have engaged in sex."

Danny realized he almost blew his cover.

"Yes, we have, I just meant not like this, today was special."

"What got into you? You have never had this much enthusiasm when we make love. Have you been watching porn? Because if you have, you have my blessings. You have learned a few new moves with that left hand."

"No, No, I.... Um, wanted to surprise you with the new me."

Sarah was all smiles as she asked if they could clear the weekend schedule and stay in bed all weekend?

"I have no problem with that." declared Brandon A.K.A. Danny.

The weekend went as planned. Sarah was unaware the twins had swapped places. Her drive back to Columbia, South Carolina went quicker than usual. She had travelled the entire distance home in a state of trance. Remembering her weekend.

Stepping off the elevator, now back in her penthouse, she looked out over the skyline of Columbia. Cell phone in hand she dialed her lover. Brandon knew Sarah had returned to Columbia and could not bear to answer the call. He let it go to voicemail.

Later his courage returned and listened to her recorded voice.

"Hello my love. Thank you for a fantastic weekend of making love to me. I am sure you are worn out and sleeping. Bye now, Love you."

Brandon paid the cab driver as he opened the cab door to the exit. He Walked to the front door of his house and without thinking almost rang the doorbell before entering his own home. It was time to collect the keys from Danny and get reassured he would never see him again. Walking into the house, he confronted his brother.

"Give me my keys Danny."

"Would you like to know how it went with me and Sarah?

"Not no, but hell no, just get out of my house."

"Danny, I do not expect to ever see you again after today."

"Hmmm, I expected her to at least call you with a lover's message." Said Danny as he started towards the door.

"Yes Danny. She called but I could not answer the phone. She left a voicemail. It was not what I wanted to listen too."

"Alright then, I need a big fat payment to disappear again."

"It is already transferred to your bank account, Brother."

"Ok Then, see you later, brother Brandon."

The next day Danny went to his bank, verified the transfer of funds from the business account to his credit card account Brandon set up. He then stepped outside and hailed a cab to the local car dealership. Bought a new vehicle and drove straight to Columbia, South Carolina to see Sarah Kill-ings.

His weekend with Sarah created a new Danny. He wanted more in life and Sarah had the ticket he needed. He could not get enough of that woman.

Arriving at Killings Insurance, LLC. Danny found the private elevator that would take him to Sarah's penthouse. Pressed the button that announced the presence of a visitor awaiting downstairs.

Sarah heard the buzzer announcing a visitor at the elevator entrance. Looking at the security monitor she was surprised to see who she thought was Brandon. Wondering why he was pausing to ride the elevator while waiting for her authorization via the security system. She granted access and Brandon AKA Danny was on his way up.

Two steps out of the elevator. Sarah was about to ask questions. No time for discussion as Danny AKA Brandon embraces her as if two lovers had been separated for years. He performed the same loving motions then almost blew his cover by asking where the bedroom was located. Seeing the hallway behind her Danny did not say a word as he lifted her up against his masculine body and headed to the hallway entrance. Finding the doorway to the bedroom he continued to carry Sarah inside.

It was a repeat performance from the weekend as the man she thought was Brandon had drove all the way to Columbia to make love to her again.

Finishing again. Sarah began questioning.

"Why have you decided to drive here to make love to me again, did you not get enough of me last weekend? You have never been this virile. This has been the eighth time since last Friday. What blue pills did your doctor prescribe you?"

"No pills Sarah, I am deeply in love with you."

"You are already in love with me Brandon, what is different?'

"Yes, I am, although I cannot stay tonight, I have to be at the docks in the morning to talk to a grouper captain that has been waiting for a meeting with me."

Danny played Brandon well. He was sure Sarah was fooled into believing he was his brother, Brandon.

At least he thought so.

Sarah was suspicious the whole weekend. She felt uncomfortable with her Brandon. Something was not kosher with him. The weekend was ending. Sarah had questions turning in her head. She began deliberating.

Why her Brandon drove from Charleston to Columbia unannounced.

Not using the security code to enter the elevator? He knows the code, why did he not use it? It was not like him. It was not his protocol to act this way. Especially waiting for the security clearance at the private elevator. He absolutely knew the 4-digit code. She watched through the large windows of the penthouse as he drove out of the parking garage and embarked on the two-hour drive back to Charleston, South Carolina.

Sarah decided to call him once he was an hour away from Columbia, knowing CarPlay would not distract him while driving and a text would be dangerous to view at night.

Brandon's phone rings.

Electing to answer the special ring he selected for Sarah's number.

"Hello Sarah, What's up?"

"I was calling to ask how your drive is going, are you getting tired?"

Brandon was confused by Sarah's questioning. He did not know Danny had pulled another fast one on him. Assuming his brother made some quick decision without informing him. Brandon had to adlib it quickly.

"I really have no answer to your question Sarah, I am fine, why do you ask if I am tired?"

"You should know why, you left my penthouse an hour ago."

Silence fills the phone's speaker; there is no sound, no speech, nothing. Brandon is at a loss for words. He must think of a response quickly.

"You know Sarah I have not been myself lately and I cannot put my finger on it."

"Don't play dumb with me mister, you know where to put your fingers."

Again, Brandon can only guess what happened from her statement. Trying diligently to play along and avoid a catastrophe, he replied, jokingly.

"Yes, ma'am I sure do."

"Oh, you southerners and that ma'am thing." She thought to herself.

Sarah decided to end it there. Not wanting to push the issue any further and said goodnight to Brandon.

Brandon ended the call on his phone just as Sarah ended it with him.

The thoughts of Danny and his antics had continued, completely caught off guard with Sarah's questioning. He deliberated calling Danny to extract the details of what he had just finished doing to him and not only him but to Sarah as well.

Danny's phone rings.

"Hello Brandon, what do you want?

"Where have you been Danny? Do not lie to me. Where have you been?"

"With Sarah of course."

"Why did you drive to Columbia to see her? We agreed to one weekend only."

"Yea, you see Brandon I just could not get enough of her."

"Danny this is irresponsible of you and typical of your uneducated…"

Danny hung up on Brandon before he could finish berating him. He had a smile on his face. He did his brother wrong, and he knew it. It was a feeling of the ultimate power over him.

I Am You Now.

Brandon was furious.

Brandon could not wait for his brother Danny to return to Charleston. He would make plans to confront him about his actions tomorrow.

Leaving his office, he ventured out to the wharf where his fleet of shrimp boats we moored. In one hand was a glass of ice, in the other a bottle of bourbon. Sipping and pouring and walking the wharf back and forth. The evening had come. The dim bulbs of the outdated lighting provided barely enough amber light to see the edge of the boards on which he was walking. The half-moon was overhead as it reflected its presence up from the shiny surface of the waves below his feet.

Carefully he stepped. The boards were worn out and weathered from storm after storm. One inaccurately placed footstep would cause him to swim to shore.

Brandon had reached the end of the old path of wooden boards many sailors before him used daily fairing materials and their catches to and from the large ships.

Reaching the end of the wharf he stood in silence listening to the waves crash into the wooden pylons of the worn-out rickety pier built many years ago.

Thinking "these boards need replacing" as each step sounded off with a grinding noise of loose boards and rusty nails from beneath his feet.

Reaching the end of his walk, he once again lifted his empty glass and began pouring another round for himself from a now, empty bottle. He leaned his head back to take another sip. Looking up at the dark moonlit sky. He could count the stars looking back at him.

Bringing the glass to his lips. He takes another sip of bourbon.

The bourbon was now warm, the ice had melted, with this last sip he felt the bourbon burning his esophagus as it slid into his stomach. He was feeling the bourbon's neurotoxic effects on his body and equilibrium.

Finishing his drink, he could hear the faint sound of footsteps signaling someone was approaching from the other end of the wharf behind him, nearing his position at a terribly slow pace.

His mind pondered who that could be, a boat captain returning from a night in the town? They often slept on the boats in leu of taking a chance on driving home intoxicated. Some Captains lived several miles from the boats and the lifestyle they dearly loved.

The slow pace of the approaching person convinced him his assumption may be correct.

The footsteps continue at the same slow cadence. The sound of the boards increased in volume as they closed the gap on him. Brandon's mind began to consider the obvious as he refused to believe his thoughts and stared off at the end of the wharf.

He was hoping for someone other than his brother as his self-questioning quickly entered his head. If this is the law coming. He might as well give up peacefully. No one needs to get shot tonight.

The footsteps were now a short distance behind him. Brandon raises both arms to show he was not armed or a danger to the person approaching him. He had convinced himself it was an officer of the law coming to arrest him for the fraud scheme he manufactured.

One last question rolled around in his head.

Who turned him in?

“Do you mind if I finish off my bourbon before you handcuff me” Brandon requested in a loud voice.

Silence is a dangerous thing when you are convinced you are cornered.

The person behind him remained silent as Brandon announced.

“Alright now, I will take the last sip, and I am all yours.”

Brandon tossed the empty bottle off the end of the wharf, watching it crashes into the water below. He swallowed the last bit of bourbon from his glass. Another bitterness of alcohol bit into him as his mouth contorted as if he bit a sour apple.

Brandon’s throat had merely cleared itself of bourbon when he decided to turn around and meet his fate.

It was not the law.

Standing in front of him was a silhouette of a man. His face blackened out from the moon setting behind him. Brandon could not tell who this was. The person stood silently, without motion, looking at Brandon.

“Who are you and what do you want? Are you law enforcement? Are you here to arrest me? If you are, then do it now will you!”

Brandon shouted questions quickly to the unknown figure with an assertive commanding drunken voice.

“Calm down Brandon. It is me, your brother Danny. I figured you would be out here. You were not in your office, but your vehicle was still in the parking lot.”

Violent rage began to take over Brandon’s inebriated posture. He was no longer the calm man waiting for handcuffs that would change his world forever.

He began shouting.

“I cannot believe what you did to me Danny, what are you thinking? Sarah does not deserve this from me or you. Better yet either of us. I agreed to accept one weekend and that was all I was willing to accept. Now, tonight I get a call from her that ‘I’ had just left her place in Columbia. You owe me a good explanation.”

A moment of pause filled the encounter before Danny began to speak.

“Calmly Danny began to speak, Brandon, I have come to a decision regarding our agreement and regarding Sarah.”

Brandon was losing his composure as alcohol was taking control of his thoughts. Anger was now controlling his emotions.

He began to yell louder at Danny.

“What do you mean, you have come to a decision? Who do you think you are? You are incapable of making decisions on your own. I have been making decisions for you, every day of your pathetic life.”

“That you have; Brandon and it is my fault for being lazy enough to let you do so. It made my life easier, and you enjoyed being a control freak, playing the smart one.”

Brandon took a stumbling step towards Danny. The alcohol had full control of his motor functions. Clinching the glass in his hand he wanted to brandish it against Danny’s skull.

Instead, he stopped and asked.

“You must have some set of balls, using your lifeless brain to risk driving all the way back to Charleston. One big set of stupidity if nothing else to confront me out here on the wharf."

Danny could not find the strength to tell Brandon his plan.

Brandon, tired of waiting yelled.

"SPIT IT OUT DANNY, TELL ME WHAT IS THIS DECISION OF YOURS?"

With that outburst from Brandon, Danny revealed his plan.

"I am putting our agreement on hold. I am not comfortable with being dead, Brandon! I need my life back. It is your turn to be Danny for a while. I will be seeing Sarah next month. You are the one who will stay away. No contact with Sarah at all. I will be with her, not you."

"I am assuming your identity" I am you now."

The two men stood facing each other. Brandon could not control his anger any longer. Lunging at Danny. The glass held with his tightly clinched fist was now heading towards Danny's temple. With one swift move Danny ducked low. Brandons fury filled momentum missed its target, causing him to lose balance and plunge into the salt water below.

Danny moved quickly to look over the side of the pier. Brandon had surfaced gasping for air. Grabbing the emergency life ring from a pylon, he threw it down to Brandon.

"I hope the cold salt water sobers you up." he shouted.

"Swim over to the ladder and get yourself together, I am out of here. I will call you tomorrow."

Brandon returned to work the next day. Opening the door to his office, Danny is sitting in his office chair behind his desk with both feet propped on the desk.

Brandon slams the door closed behind him as he begins to yell at Danny.

"What are you doing here? We are going to get, caught."

Brandon calmed himself as Danny sat in the chair staring at him when he decided to speak.

"Actually, last night I thought it was the feds coming up behind me, to arrest me for the fraud I committed. I was, initially, relieved it was you until you opened your mouth with that dumb news you announced. You cannot be me

Danny, it will not work, so forget the idea, and get out of here before someone sees you."

"Brandon my brother if I walk out of here in broad daylight. Everyone will think I am you; I am DEAD! Danny is DEAD! Remember? That was your idea. And I am realizing no one believes I am alive anyway. Who they SEE! Out there, every day, is you Brandon."

"THEY SEE YOU!'

"Same build, same face. same hair. Everything is the same. Other than the fact of being right and left-handed and no one knows that except us and our parents that are now deceased."

"I say this again to you. I am you now and you cannot stop me."

Brandon stood in the office mystified at Dannys recollection of the situation, he knew he created this monster. The only problem he has now is he did not figure Danny had the brainpower to think of an alternative to all of his planning. He expected Danny to be deceased and stay that way. Instead, Danny wised up, realizing he did not need to stay dead. Danny now assumes his identity as Brandon Davies.

Especially with his beloved Sarah.

Brandon had to try and reason with Danny. In a calm voice.

"Brother please listen to me. This will not work for public appearances. Please think for a minute. We cannot be in the same proximity or seen together or in separate locations simultaneously. This will eventually throw a red flag in the air. We will get, caught."

"We, Brother, you said WE?" Let me remind you, this was your idea from the start."

Brandon broke into Danny's speech with. "May I remind YOU, Danny, you are an accomplice to this. You and Captain Charlie.

Pointing a finger from his right hand at Danny he shouted.

"So do not threaten me."

Danny quickly realized his last statement nearly caused him to spit out he was working against him already. The anger directed at Brandon nearly ruined the surveillance of the F.B.I. It would be game over too soon without more information recorded from this meeting. Calming himself he knew it was time to reveal the full details of his plan to spend a greater amount of time with Sarah.

The investigation needed Danny to spend some time with Sarah to confirm she played no part in the scheme.

Danny continued conveying his plan.

"Brandon, I am putting you on notice. Tomorrow I will be leaving for Columbia to convince Sarah to take a short vacation with me. Once that is completed. I will agree to go back to hiding. This will be my final hurrah. I swear to you, I will no longer see Sarah after this trip. With that said, I will be leaving now. Move away from the door."

"Danny, before I move and let you walk out this door. You must promise, this is the last time you will be with Sarah?"

"Yes, I promise."

"You have promised before Danny and reneged." said Brandon.

"I understand your concern, Brandon. But this time it is different. I have a plan to make it all up to you soon. Please trust me, after this trip, you will never have to deal with me again for a long time."

"I hate shaking your hand but if you are sincere then I will agree. Let us shake on it." Replied Brandon.

The two brothers shook hands as Danny stood next to Brandon, looked him in the eye, and asked.

"I need the elevator code."

Brandon sheepishly looked away and mumbled "three-six-nine-eight."

Danny then moved past his brother to exit the office doorway.

Danny unlocked his vehicle to enter the driver's door. Driving a short distance to a parking lot and found an empty parking spot. At the same time the same white unmarked van pulled into a spot next to him.

Stepping out he assumed the same role of raising his shirt for the agents to remove the audio microphone.

Just then Agent Downing pulled up beside Danny and the other agents. Rolling down his window and motioned for Danny to step closer.

"Good work son. Now let us get you to Columbia for the next leg of our investigation. You will not be wearing a wire while you are in her home. We have hacked into her TV speakers and her laptop camera including the microphone. We will be listening to everything you talk about."

"You can do all that, without her knowledge?" asked Danny.

"We can and did already. If she has any prior knowledge of fraud we will arrest her along with your brother. Do not worry, we obtained the proper warrants for surveillance of her penthouse. Just do not walk around naked in front of her open laptop."

Danny donned a ball cap he had stashed in the vehicle. Remembering what his brother said. He cannot afford to be spotted in one location while Brandon was in another. He decides to be incognito until he arrives in Columbia, South Carolina and safely in Sarah's penthouse.

Danny stopped at the hotel outside of town. His Brother decided this was the best spot for Danny to hide out. It was an old run-down forgotten flea bag establishment. Hookers and druggies hung around like flies. Begging for a handout or offering services for money.

His luggage was already packed. It was grab and go. He was off to see Sarah.

Leaning down to grab the handle of his luggage Danny noticed a sealed envelope attached to the handle with a small piece of tape.

Standing upright he stared at the luggage and the envelope attached. Reaching for the envelope he opens to read the note inside.

It was from Detective Downing.

"We secured a special room for you two at the Wilcox in Aiken, South Carolina. Surveillance equipment has already been installed in the room. The booking clerk has also been notified. Just act normally, we have taken care of everything.

Signed Agent: Clarence Downing.

Last Trip with Sarah

Brandon had enough work for the day. He struggled to concentrate on bills, paying taxes and the onslaught of calls from creditors he knew needed their money and obviously they knew he had received the insurance money for Danny's demise.

The conversations always started with condolences but quickly turned to the question of the day.

"WHERE'S THE MONEY YOU OWE ME?"

Brandon left the office, opened his car door, and started the engine. Turning his wrist, he took a quick look to check the time on his watch. His cell phone that survived the plunge into the water sounded off with the special ringtone he assigned to his Sarah.

Without any thought about his action. He retrieved it from his back pocket, used his finger to swipe the phone to answer the call.

At the same instant he realized his mistake. He knew Danny was on the way to visit Sarah.

Struggling for the words he finally mumbled into the phone three words.

"Hello my love."

"Hey Sweetie, are you coming here this weekend or am I driving down to stay with you in Charleston? I have been occupied with work and lost track of time, and I have not heard from you in a couple of days, so I have to ask. Are you ok Brandon? Is everything all right with the business?"

"I um, yes, yes, of course, I am on my way to you, my love. You should be seeing me shortly."

Brandon struggled to think of that response to Sarah's question. A brief moment had passed before he could respond.

He clinched the same fist of his right hand. The one he used in his failed attempt to take out Danny the previous night while announcing to Sarah, she should soon see his arrival in Columbia, South Carolina.

Joyously relieved her boo-thang was, headed her way. Brandon could hear Sarah's joy, and relieved she was not asked to drive to Charleston, South Carolina.

"I guess I will see you in a little while Honey, Bye now."

Brandon could only reply in kind as he ended the call. Immediately using his clinched fist to bange on the steering wheel of his car. Throwing the phone into the passenger seat he put the car in gear and drove home.

Sarah had a surprise waiting for her man. She had been in the kitchen preparing a dinner of fresh seabass almondine with asparagus and mashed potatoes. Her first home cooked meal since Robert had passed. She was moving forward, just as her therapist suggested.

Sarah was now confident in herself again. With a glowing energy, her plans were to surprise Brandon with her cooking talents.

Although it would not be Brandon stepping off the elevator.

Danny had arrived. Pressing the security code he entered the elevator. Immediately assumed the role of his brother Brandon Davies once again.

The doors were only half open as he quickly squeezed his body sideways through them. Sarah was standing in front of the elevator doors as if she were in a queue. As she did with Robert, she greeted her man coming home with a hug and a kiss.

Danny now AKA Brandon walked straight to her. Embraced her in his strong arms, lifting her from the floor, pulling her tight to his hips. She knew what was coming.

"Wait Brandon I have dinner on the stove." She mumbled while her lips were locked to his.

"I cannot wait until we have dinner Sarah, I want you, NOW!

Sarah was now being carried to the bedroom.

"Ok," was her reply as she yelled out.

"ALEXA, TURN OFF THE STOVE."

Sitting at the dining table Sarah noticed a different pattern in Brandons eating habit.

"Brandon darling is something wrong with the sea-bass? You have been taking more time to eat your food tonight and you usually finish eating before I do. You also look me in the eye while engaging in conversation. When did you start using your left hand to hold your fork?"

Danny had to think fast. He needed an explanation to settle Sarah's inquisitive questions as quickly as possible.

"Oh, babe you know how I love to use the fingers on my left hand. I am surprised you had not noticed I was ambidextrous."

Sarah broke out in laughter. The dinner wine had put her in a playful mood. She replied. I know too well what you can do with those fingers."

"Listen Sarah I was thinking we should take a trip up to Aiken, South Carolina. It is a beautiful Southern town. Well, known as a thoroughbred horse community. It has a training track for Northerners to use before the spring race circuit starts. They are hosting a steeple-chase sporting event this weekend. What do you think?"

"That is a great idea. After dinner and another round with you. I will pack a bag."

"I booked a room at the Wilcox. It was an internationally known inn during the Aiken winter colony heydays. It is a magnificent building with a late 18th century architectural design. It is, listed on the National Register of Historic Places in 1982."

"Oh, wow this sounds exciting. You are becoming quite the history buff. I had no idea if you have an interest in history or horses. You had me at horses were included in this trip. I am impressed; have you have been planning this for some time?"

"Yes, I have, you know I would do anything for you Sarah."

Leaning back in his chair he looked into Sarah's eyes. It is our time; I think those dishes will have to wait."

Sarah's eyes widened as she smiled, with a playful reply "Again?"

Pushing her chair back.

"I agree, last one in the bedroom washes dishes."

Danny, AKA Brandon tried to stand quickly to beat Sarah to the bedroom. She was too fast. He knew he was getting the best and the hard end of the deal at the same time.

Aiken, South Carolina is a 50-minute drive from the penthouse. Checking into the Wilcox Hotel. Danny tricked Sarah into strolling away from him momentarily as he provided Brandon Davies' information to the desk clerk.

"Everything is now, taken care of Mr. Davies. Here are your keys. You can go straight up to your room."

Sarah returned to her imposture of a boyfriend.

"We are now, checked in. I am hungry, how about you, my love?"

The clerk overheard Danny's question and broke in on their conversation to recommend.

"We have dinner here if you prefer to stay. or there is a local eatery I recommend that is a short walk from here. They have great burgers."

"I think that would be fantastic. What is the name of the place?" asked Danny.

"It is, called 'City Billiards' an old school billiards hall established in 1957. They have a slogan on the door windows that states."

'The Best Cheeseburger you will ever Eat.'

"Alrighty, let us go there. They must know what they are doing if they have been in business that long." replied Sarah.

Walking back to the Wilcox Sarah once again noticed the man she thought was Brandon had lost his skills of being a gentleman.

"Brandon, what happened to chivalry? she asked.

"I'm sorry Sarah what are you referring to?"

"You Brandon! You always escort a lady down the street with her on the inside away from traffic. You were a gentleman before this weekend and now I am on the streetside. Why are you being so different? You have never treated me this way."

"Sarah my darling I do not know what has come over me. I have been off my game, please accept my apologies."

"You did say something along those lines earlier when I called asking if you were coming here or not."

Danny had no words to respond to that statement. It was not him she talked to, and Brandon did not call to inform him she had phoned him asking about the plans for their weekend rendezvous.

His brain called out.

"Touché to you Brandon."

A short distance from the Hotel Sarah was still walking alongside of her man, still on the street side as he never caught on to the meaning behind expressing her concerns for the change in the way he was acting.

The steps up to the wooden front doors of the Wilcox Hotel are made from old bricks laid down years ago. A showpiece from a dated time when concrete had not been, used for construction as much as it is today. The roots from the old trees are the bricks only keepers during their tenure as steps. Time offers a protrusion of a few rows, as the roots push them up from their chosen resting spot. Each brick has a story to tell of a hand that put them where they stand today.

Sarah had reached the doorway. She stood for a moment, waiting for her new prince charming to reach around her to open them as a gentleman should.

"Are you planning to open the door for me or should I ask some other Southerner to do it for me?"

"Here, let me get that for you Sarah."

"Brandon, you are in another world tonight. Has the honeymoon worn off with you already?"

"No, my love, not at all. Please forgive me. How about you go up to the room and get comfortable and I will go order us some Ice-cream brought up to us?"

"No thank you. I need a cocktail at the bar. You need to work on how to treat a lady before we return to the room. I know what is on your mind, mister."

Sarah took a seat at the bar, looked over her shoulder to see if her Brandon had followed suit. She was happy to see he found the empty chair next to her.

The bartender appeared asking for their drink order.

Sarah turned to look into Danny AKA Brandons eyes then asked.

"Are you going to order for us darling?"

Danny had no clue what her favorite drink was. He was clueless. So, he improvised to get a feel for her preferred drink.

"If I may ask Sarah, would you prefer wine or bourbon tonight?"

"Wine will be fine."

Danny was relieved. He knew what wine she drank at home for dinner before they left. Looking away from Sarah to address the bartender.

"I will have a Dewars on the rocks and my lady will have a glass of your finest Rose'."

"DEWARS?" Sarah asked.

Danny could see a tear forming in the corner of her eye. Grabbing a bar napkin he handed it to Sarah.

Sarah thanked him for his generosity as she wiped the liquid from her cheek.

"Sarah my love, I am terribly sorry if my actions tonight have caused you this much stress. I did not intend to make you cry."

"Oh, sweetie your actions are not the reason for my emotional behavior. I shed these tears for my late husband. You see I have never told you I met him at a bar. He was drinking DEWARS on the rocks when we met."

"Thank you for sharing this with me. I know how devastating losing someone you love is. Those experimental ultralight planes are truly dangerous. There is no license required to operate one and no FAA inspections before a person goes flying in them."

Sarah was still collecting her tears in the napkin when she turned to Danny, the man she thought was Brandon. In a soft voice she asked.

"How did you know it was an experimental plane? I have not been able to talk about it to anyone since the accident happened?"

Danny was now in a pinch. How to express to Sarah his knowledge of her past. The few meetings with agent Clarence Downing included one meeting with Carley attending.

She provided as much information as she could about Her boss's life, with Brandon and a few notes of her marriage to Robert. Including how he had perished in an experimental plane crash into a semi-truck on interstate 20 East of Columbia, South Carolina.

Staring into Sarah's eyes he had to think quickly. Just as he was about to abort his mission, he remembered Carley giving him a side note of advice.

"If you slip up and reveal what you know about Robert before she has a chance to talk about him. Just say you heard it from the news channel that reported it."

"Sarah! It was all over the news channels when it happened. I know all about it."

"Oh, yes of course it was. Sorry for asking a dumb question."

"Listen Sarah, what do you say we head to the room and just sit around and talk tonight. Tell me more about the cases you are working on. I want to learn how you get involved in fraud cases. How does that sound?"

"That is a clever idea. Let's get to know each other on this trip. It seems all we know about each other is intimate part of a relationship."

"I am hoping you don't view that as a bad thing my darling Sarah."

"Oh no, quite contrary, it is your best attribute."

Back in the comfort of the hotel room Sarah revealed everything about her. The time she spent as a journalist. Her time with Robert and the crash.

Danny A.K.A. Brandon listened intently without saying a word or cutting into her conversation.

Sarah was getting tired and so was Danny. He stood declaring he was going to take a shower while she composed herself.

Taking off his clothes, he threw his trousers on the bed and walked naked to the bathroom.

Sarah looked over at his pants. His cell phone had come out of his back pocket. She had been skeptical of this encounter and needed confirmation it was Brandon she was sleeping with.

Sarah picked up her phone and dialed Brandon as she kept her eye on the phone sticking out of the pocket. It was ringing but not on the phone on the bed. Quickly she hung up before the real Brandon could answer.

Brandon's phone was sitting face down on his nightstand. He had just walked into his bedroom. Standing by his bed he experienced the heart pounding emotion as he recognized her ringtone.

Something was not right with the man she was with. Her mind went viral thinking. Who is this man in the shower. He looks like Brandon but acts differently.

"I have to confront him before it gets worse. I need an explanation."

Danny A.K.A. Brandon returns from the shower as Sarah is ready to interrogate.

Brandon is closing the distance with only a towel around his waist. Sarah can see the muscular chest, facial hair, his eyes, and other features. She is in full journalist, detective mode as she reaches out with her arm placing her hand on who she thinks is Brandon's chest. Stopping him instantly.

"I have a question for you Brandon? You are Brandon, are you not?

"Sarah, my love what is going on here?"

"I need to show you something."

Sarah, holding her phone in hand waiting for her "Brandon" to return from the shower, initiates a call to his number as she turns the face of her phone towards Danny A.K.A. Brandon to prove she made the call.

"I am dialing you; Your phone is there in your pants on the bed. It is not ringing."

Danny is in a hot seat but remembers his brother falling into the water from the wharf.

"Sarah, I recently dropped my phone in the salt water off the wharf. This is a new phone and a new number."

"Ok. just checking."

Sarah knew he was lying. She had called Brandons number before he arrived. He did answer her call.

It Is Time to Tell Her

It is now Monday. Sarah passes Carley on the way to her office, giving out the normal pleasantries of,

"Good morning, how was your weekend?"

Any given day this sweet Southern Carley would be full of spunk and vinegar just waiting for the opportunity to tell someone about her weekend. Sarah assessed long ago it was a southern thing and listened to Carley rant about herself, her husband, or her children's antics.

Today was different, Carley was different.

"Come in my office and talk to me Carley. You can bring any news with you about that claim I assigned to you."

Carley, reached for the claims folder. Stood up slowly taking a deep breath before looking back at some of the other employees in the fraud division. Some turned away shaking their heads. Other employees who were helping her with the discovery knew she had a lot of weight on her shoulders. They displayed thumbs up as support. One of her assistants pointed it out to Carley.

"You have to do this Carley; It's time to tell her."

It was her job to present the shocking news. Carley delayed telling Sarah for months. She was now forced to show the cards she was holding.

Carley entered Sarah's office and closed the door behind her. Sarah looked up dismayed as Carley never closed the door.

"Miss Killings. I have some."

"Stop with the formal addressing Carley, you know I am 'Sarah' to you."

"Yes ma'am, you asked me to investigate this fifty-million-dollar life insurance claim. The team discovered who the beneficiary was that received the money."

"Good Job, Carley, who is it?

"If you do not mind waiting here, I must go to the break room. There are two agents from the F.B.I. here waiting to talk to you."

"Wait! What? The F.B.I.? Carley, why are they here? Is it something bad about Robert? The estate? This business?"

“They can explain everything. They asked to be notified when you get into your office. I do not possess the same information they have.”

“What information do you have Carley?” Shouted Sarah.

“They have more to tell you than I do.”

“I swear Carly if you have been holding information about this investigation. Wait! Is this about the plane crashing into the semi-trailer on the interstate? Am I getting sued?”

“Ma’am please calm down. Everything will be explained in detail by the agents that are here. I will be here in the office with them for addition consultation if needed.”

Carley paused as the two women stared at each other for a brief moment before Carley spoke out.

“I need to go get them right now.”

“Go Carley, go get them, now!”

Carly escorted the two agents into Sarah’s office. Without saying anything, they motioned to sit in the chairs in front of Sarah’s desk.

Sarah began turning her office chair away from the window to look at the two agents sitting in front of her. The conversation with Carly caused her to reflect on the passing of her prince charming.

Sarah had been crying as she attempted to wipe tears from her cheeks.

"Are you ok Sarah? Asked Carly. I can ask them to come back another day if you are uncomfortable speaking with them today?"

Sarah heard Carly but chose to ignore her question as she looked straight at the two agents. She began talking frantically about her Robert and the crash.

"I did not know he was flying in that plane. Before I left him on an assignment with the magazine, I assure you, I reminded him of the risks he did not need to take."

Sarah was pounding her index finger on the desk to make her point and continued vocalizing her opinion.

"He never took that kind of risk before that day. NEVER! I am telling you the truth. That trucker's family has been, compensated very well."

Carly made several attempts to stop Sarah with hand gestures to stop talking.

Sarah ignored her attempts. Brushing her motions way with her own hand gestures as she continued to ramble incoherently at the two agents in front of her. They were amused at Sarah's tirade of endless words that had no bearing on why they were there. Without her even noticing they turned to look at each other in astonishment.

Agent Downing raised both hands in the air to stop Sarah's rambling.

"Miss Sarah Killings, can you stop for a minute and listen to us. I am a special agent Clarence Downing and my assistant agent with me today is Clarissa Stevenson, we are with the F.B.I. Charleston division. We are investigating the proclaimed death of a Danny Davies. Does that name ring a bell with you? I understand you know Brandon Davies, his brother from Charleston, South Carolina."

"Yes, yes, I do know Brandon, why do you ask? What? A brother you say. Brandon does not have a brother. What does your visit today have to do with him or them if I may ask?"

"Miss Killings"

Sarah interrupted the special agent.

"Please agent Downing, call me Sarah."

“Ok, Sarah if it gives you comfort? The F.B.I. received a call from Charleston public safety about a couple of months ago. Our undercover bartender was overpouring an offshore commercial boat captain one weekend at a local bar. It was Bloody Mary Sunday I believe.

This drunk Captain commences to tell our young agent moonlighting as a bartender about a fraud scheme he was involved in.”

Sarah settled down when she realized their presence was not about her Robert or the crash involving the trucker.

“Ok, what does a drunk sailor have to do with me and our claim?” asked Sarah.

“I am getting to that Sarah, if I may continue.”

“Yes of course Clarence, my apologies for interrupting you.”

Clarence paused for a few seconds as he looked at Sarah.

“As I was saying, the captain had information on the disappearance of Danny Davies. who was reported missing and lost at sea by his brother when Danny Davies did not return to port after an offshore fishing trip. The accident and loss of a twin brother made National news headlines for a week. His body and boat were never found at the time.

"Again, I have to ask you Clarence, what information are you bringing me that this agency does not already know? What is the relevance to us?""

"Sarah, please be patient" asked Carley.

"As I was saying, the F.B.I. sometimes gets involved in the investigation if local authorities and coast guard were the agencies searching for Mr. Davies are unable to locate a body. But this time the Brother Danny Davies and his accomplish, a boat Captain named Charlie came to us to confess the scheme concocted to fraud your company."

"Wait, Back Up a minute. The brother is supposed to have perished in an accident, and he is still alive, and he comes to you to confess, beforehand? am I hearing this correctly?"

"Yes. We set up an operation with Danny Davies and Captain Charlie to gain more information and confirm their story. It seems when you buy a boat captain alcoholic drinks, he will not shut up."

"I'm listening to you Clarence, what does Killings Insurance need to do at this point to help in this investigation?"

"AGAIN, let me finish Please, Ms. Killings."

Carley was sitting next to agent Clarence Downing. She knew the unwelcome news was about to hit Sarah like a brick. She also knew Danny Davies's brother was none other than Brandon Davies. Sarah's new love.

"The information I am about to tell you Sarah may be unsettling to you. The twin brother who reported Danny Davies missing is Brandon Davies, your boyfriend. We have had all three of you under surveillance for several weeks now. I want you to know, the agency does not consider you as a suspect in the fraud plan. Our investigation into this crime strictly surrounds the actions of Brandon and Danny Davies at this time, we consider you and your company Killings LLC a victim of his crime."

Sarah slumped in her chair. Beginning to cry. She had a feeling that something was wrong with Brandon all along.

FBI agent Clarence Downing asked Sarah to give them a statement in her own words describing her activity with Brandon Davies from the time they met up to the last weekend they spent together.

Agent Clarrisa Stevenson scribbled Sarah's statement on a note pad as she described her relationship with Brandon, specifically how they met and the activities they engaged in.

Sarah conveyed how she recently became suspicious of Brandon. Giving details of their travels and always seeing Brandon engage with a man giving him money. She was convinced it was the same guy but could not confirm it.

"Is there anything else you can tell me about either of them?"

"I could but you really do not need intimate details, I will keep those to myself if you don't mind."

"We do not need anything of that nature, ma'am." said agent Stevenson."

Sarah relied, "You must be Southern young lady?"

Agent Downing decided to ask Carley if she preferred to break the sad news, they all knew about Danny pretending to be Brandon.

"I am sorry agent downing I Think you should have that honor." Replied Carley.

"Alright then, Sarah this will be a hard pill to swallow but here it is. You have been dating Brandon, right?"

“Yes” Replied Sarah

“Well, you have also been dating his identical twin brother Danny Davies. He has been stepping in pretending to be his brother, your boyfriend Brandon.”

Sarah could not find the words to respond to this revelation from agent Downing. She suspected there was a problem with Brandon, but she could not find the underlying cause of it, besides, she was having the time of her life and did not want to upset the relationship. Instead, she went with the flow.

“Silence cannot fill the air; It does not exist as a substance. Although it is, always referred to as being, so thick a person could cut it with a knife.”

Finally, Sarah spoke.

“What do you need me to do?”

“Will you wear a wire to help us get the two of them together or close proximity to make an arrest?” Asked agent Downing.

“Unfortunately, a wire is out of the question, now that I am convinced there are two of them, I am not sure now, which one is more handsy with me than the other. Honestly, one is quite irresistible, dam hard to tell them apart. So, no that will not work,

AT ALL! Sarah replied with a chuckle.

"T.M.I., Sarah, T.M.I., We are working on a plan to record the two of them together with you. If you cannot wear a wire to record the conversation, we will need access to your residence to install listening hardware to record any conversation that can be useful in their apprehension and of course used in a court of law for a conviction. Just so, you are aware, once arrested, your company will never see this con artist again outside of a prison cell. It will be your company's responsibility to initiate separate legal action to recover a return of money they frauded from Killings Insurance, LLC."

Sarah was still silent as she listened to Agent Downing's finishing remarks.

"In closing please note. You will see them arrested and standing trial in a court of law and if convicted, sent to prison for a long time. My question to you now, Ms. Killings, are you ok with this?"

Sarah could not answer right away as a few more tears had streaked down her cheeks. Her throat swelled preventing her vocal cords from articulating the words floating around in her head. This was a difficult decision. She knew it was the end of her relationship with Brandon and the short, intimate relationship Danny provided. Sarah nurtured deep feelings for a single man and now knew she was dealing with two separate lovers. Her feelings could not get in the way of the law.

She had slumped in her chair.

Carley and Special agent Clarence Downing sat silent, giving Sarah a moment to reflect on her decision to help convict her lovers.

Raising her hand to her face wiping the tears from her cheeks. Sarah nodded her head to acknowledge what she must do. It was the largest fraud claim Killings Insurance LLC had ever paid out. Someone needed to be held accountable.

Sarah was finally able to reply with a soft voice.

"Yes, I am in. Get back to me with the details soon."

Agent Downing spoke.

"Thank you for your time, Sarah, I will reach out when we are ready. For now, I leave you to your thoughts."

"I do have one last request of you Sarah. This will be the most difficult part I have to ask of you. In order for us to convict, it will be absolutely necessary for you to function as normally as you can when around them. Can you do that?"

"You can count on me agent Downing. Now I am upset with them. Have a wonderful day. Carly will escort you out."

Sarah informed Carley she needed to get away for the day and lie in bed to cry for a while.

"I need to think this through." she said.

Sarah had a lot of respect for special agent Downing. His presentation of evidence was informative and to the point.

Carley calls Sarah after two days of being a no show at work.

"Sarah, how are you feeling honey?"

"I am getting myself back together now. I will be in tomorrow morning."

"Great news Sarah, I am glad to hear you are better, I know it has been a couple rough days. Did the F.B.I. install the bugs and video surveillance cameras in your penthouse?"

"They are not bugs Carley; you have been watching too many spy movies."

"The correct terminology Carley is,

{Audio recording devices} and yes, they are, covertly installed."

"Yippee," yelled Carley.

"Too much excitement Carly, tone it down a little, you have more excitement for catching thieves than spy thriller."

"Yes, ma'am"

The sun was setting as Sarah poured herself a cocktail, to watch it disappear from the western horizon. Nightfall had arrived when the security system alerted her of a visitor at the private elevator. To her surprise the security monitor once again displayed Brandon at the entrance. Or was this Danny she quizzed. There was only one way to find out and that was to let him in.

Acknowledging the security system, letting him enter the elevator and ride it to the penthouse. She knew how each man would react to greeting her as soon as they stepped off the elevator. Each had his way of approaching her, Brandon was subtle and gentle with slow kisses. Danny was vigorously aggressive from the time he grabbed her to the end of the best sex she had ever had.

Waiting for the elevator to reach the top floor she could not help but want Danny to be the one to step out of the elevator. What could hurt having one last encounter with the man that put her on a pedestal of excitement. Sex with Danny was a rocket ship ride to the moon and back.

The doors were opening, Sarah was quickly getting aroused as Danny swiftly walked up, lifted her in his strong arms, kissing her lips with a feverish passion all the way to the bedroom. Again, it was the probing with those fingers on his left hand that left no doubt it was Danny.

The F.B.I. had set up their listening and video surveillance equipment one floor below Sarah's penthouse. Watching and listening to everything from start to finish. They also knew from the heavy sounds coming from Sarah it had to be Danny in her bedroom.

Sarah could hear her phone begin to vibrate a short distance away. "Excuse me a minute D……um Brandon I need to check my text message. I left my phone in the kitchen; You can take a shower while I figure if that message is important.

Sigmund Freud extensively studied the inner workings of the mind. He concluded that people would be thinking of one word to say but unintentionally say a different word. He coined this slip as.

'The Freudian slip' which Sarah caught the mistake a second before she spoke Danny's name.

Danny may have been a fantastic world-class lover but lacked the intelligence to realize Sarah had almost said his name.

Sarah picked up the phone to look at the message. It was agent Downing, with an urgent warning. Brandon had pulled into Killings Insurance's underground garage.

Sarah waited to hear the water running from the walk-in shower then quickly dialed agent Downing.

"What is he doing here?" she asked.

"As I mentioned, we have them both under surveillance. The agent assigned to follow him let us know he was on the way here."

"Why are you letting me know this NOW? Mr. Downing.

"You were, occupied for the last hour ma'am, we are letting you know, Brandon is now in the elevator. We are ready to come arrest them as soon as we record the confession. It will be up to you to figure out how to make that happen, you have the opportunity to have them in the same room at the same time. Make it happen! We cannot coach you through it. There is no time left at this point. Just make it happen."

Confession Time

Sarah set her phone down on the counter of the kitchen center island. Intentionally failing to end the call. Agent Downing assumed she wanted him to listen in and kept the call connected.

Sarah took a moment as she leaned back against the kitchen counter. Just as Brandon exited the elevator. Sarah had left her robe open on purpose. Exposing her breast and feminine part covered only with lace panties for Brandon.

Her plan worked as Brandon came to a stop boasting a large smile as he gazed at her beauty.

Sarah closed her robe slowly tying the fabric with a double knot.

Sarah quietly asked.

"What do I owe the pleasure of your visit Brandon?"

Brandon stuttered for the first time.

"I, well, I came to talk to you. I have a confession to make."

Sarah perked up as she replied sarcastically.

"Really now! I am all, ears, Brandon."

"It can wait until you finish showering, I hear the water running and you are half naked under your robe, I will be happy to scrub your back."

"You should not make assumptions Brandon; appearances can be deceiving. Playfully she asks, please tell me what it is you want to discuss?"

Sarah kept her distance from Brandon. As he moved closer to Sarah, she decided to move to the other side of the kitchen island, placing it between them.

"Go on I'm listening."

Brandon stopped, dismayed at Sarah's defensive move, he cautiously approached the kitchen island. Still puzzled at Sarah, he could hear the creaking sound of water valves making when someone is turning off the water in a shower. He looked back over his shoulder towards the location of the bathroom then looked back at Sarah.

Brandon stood quietly, staring at Sarah, blinking as Sarah shrugged her shoulder and cocked her head slightly.

Brandon never looked back to see who it was approaching. It was Deja' Vu as his brother Danny slowly exited from the hallway with the same pace used to reach his brother on the Wharf.

Danny's head lowered, as he attempted to tie a towel around his waist.

Danny looked up from his towel and came to an abrupt halt a mere two steps behind his brother, Brandon.

Danny quickly turned his focus on Sarah behind the kitchen island, then looked back towards his brother as his fists were beginning to clinch tightly ready for a fight.

He abruptly asks.

"Why are you here Brandon? You were in a meeting with the employees at the packaging company."

"Brandons eyes were, fixed onto Sarah as he answered his brother. I cancelled the meeting, Danny, I am not going to ask you what you are doing here, especially naked in my girlfriend's house."

Brandon paused for a few seconds after questioning his brother then mumbled while gently moving his head side to side.

"I cannot believe this is happening."

Sarah was relieved, Brandon and Danny controlled their urge to fight each other over her. Instead, Brandon lowered his head in shame.

Danny showed the same remorse. It was all over, Sarah had them cornered. Just as agent Downing requested. Both men were now in the same proximity with Sarah.

Sarah was now in a position to control the situation. If she could get either one of the brothers to openly admit they committed fraud this charade would finally terminate.

Wanting to scream at them both with every bit of rage and anger. She needed answers before the F.B.I. would barge in with the arrest warrant for Brandon and Danny as well.

The first round of questions concentrated on the decision to have a threesome without discussing it with her.

"Brandon, Danny, whose decision was it to pretend to be each other and sleep with me?"

Danny held the towel with one hand as he raised the other in recognition, he was the one. But to her surprise, Brandon, not able to see Danny behind him, raised his hand as soon as Danny was in the air.

Slamming both of her palms on the marble countertop, she screamed.

"BOTH OF YOU?"

Sarah decided to soften her tone. Knowing special agent Clarence Downing was still listening to the conversation. She begins with.

"Thank you both for the great times. Both of you managed yourselves like gentlemen. Well not so much Danny. Each of you provided me with love and affection, even though you are identical twins, it was not hard to figure out that something was wrong.

So, I played along to see how far this would go. You were so intent on fooling me, you failed to discuss the differences between you.

First of all, let me point out the flaws in your plan.

Investigative reporting has taught me there is a clue to every puzzle and that every scheme has a fatal flaw.

Brandon and Danny had a look of surprise on their faces as they turned to look at each other.

Sarah was amused at their ignorance. All they could do was stand in silence before her as she continued to explain.

Brandon you are right-hand dominant, and Danny is left-hand dominant, she added, while mustering a sinister grin, I love what you can do with the fingers on your left-hand Danny."

Danny began to smile as Sarah SNAPPED! her fingers to bring him to attention.

"You can wipe the smile off your face right now." said Sarah in a stern voice. "I need to finish."

"You have different habits while eating dinner with me. Brandon, you are more talkative and Danny, all you care about is eating. Intelligent conversation with the two of you has a completely different spectrum. There is more but I will not bore you with the details of intimacy."

Sarah could not help but throw a pitiful party for them.

"Look at you two. Nothing to say?"

Sarah had to play dumb about the plan they obviously created together. She had to get it out of them somehow. But how?

Sarah was still in control of the moment as she continued her questioning. He octave level ascending with each question volleyed at them.

"Ok, let us start from the beginning. Why did you two decide to take advantage of me?

You tried to fool me into thinking I had one lover."

"What were you thinking?"

"Why did you decide to do this to me?"

"When did you come up with this plan to deceive me?"

"WHO WAS THE MASTERMIND BEHIND THIS PLAN?"

Brandon raised his hand as Danny pointed a finger at his brother using his left hand. Still, no verbal words were spoken for the confirmation the F.B.I. requested.

Sarah snapped at Danny,

"I hope you washed those fingers in the shower; now will you please go put your clothes back on so we can finish this conversation."

Danny left the room as Sarah continued to interrogate Brandon.

"While Danny is putting his clothes on Brandon, you can indulge me with the reason you did this to me."

Brandon stood silent, not a single word uttered from his mouth as Sarah's anger grew with intensity second by second.

She was not getting the confession the F.B.I. needed.

Sarah could no longer hold the anger inside her as she decided to lash out, pounding her fist on the kitchen island, with a loud raging voice she shouted.

"GIVE ME ONE GOOD REASON YOU DID THIS TO ME, BRANDON!"

Sarah quickly reasoned if she shouted Brandon's name loud enough it would spark an equally reactive response from him.

It worked several times in her career when she needed an informant to talk. Even if they were afraid for their life.

Like clockwork, it worked flawlessly.

Brandon was unable to control himself after her outburst as his anger bested his emotions. He shouted his response back at Sarah with vengeance.

"I HAD FIFTY MILLION REASONS! SARAH."

Slowly Brandon reiterated his point.

"I, HAD, FIFTY, MILLION, REASONS."

Brandon did not stop there. He continued shouting out every detail of the plan he set in motion. Starting with taking Danny fishing.

Convincing him to agree to sink the boat into Gulf-stream where it would never be found. How he knew captain Charlie needed money for his grandkid's college and chuckled at how easy it was for Bribe Charlie to pick up Danny, taking him to the hill.

He continued explaining how his company was failing financially and needed a cash infusion to survive and how he knew his brother was dumb enough to go along with the scheme when he told him how much life insurance was worth.

Brandon paused to collect himself. Turning his head slightly to see better. He could hear footsteps coming up behind him. Without totally looking back, he knew it was Danny.

Danny was now standing next to his brother.

"You thought I was dumb enough to play along, But I am smart enough to ask Charlie to disclose information to the bartender. You thought I was dumb enough not to tell the F.B.I. everything I knew about your plan to defraud Sarah's company out of the insurance money. Captain Charlie and I suspected the bartender was a federal agent. He kept asking questions pertaining to the plan. You really thought you would get away with swindling a company out of fifty million dollars, didn't you?

You are my twin brother, and I love you, but I had to give you up. What you did was wrong Brandon. Neither Captain Charlie nor I wanted to take the chance of spending the rest of our life in prison."

Brandon took a moment to reply to Danny.

"Danny, I told you, I did this for us. I had to do it to save the business."

Hearing Brandon confess, Clarence Downing ended the call with Sarah's phone and gathered all the agents waiting at the elevator door just one floor below the penthouse.

Having been given the security code beforehand that would allow the elevator to access the penthouse floor. He entered the four-digit number, and the doors opened for the ten agents coming to arrest Brandon Davies for insurance fraud.

Before all the F.B.I. agents could load themselves in the elevator to come up to the penthouse. Sarah had a minute to ask Danny one question.

"Do you mean to tell me Danny Davies; you were working with the F.B.I. this entire time? Why did you keep that a secret from me?"

Danny took a single step towards Sarah as he answered her question.

"Agent Clarence Downing asked me not to. He needed to make sure you and Brandon were not working together to defraud your company out of that much money. His profilers knew couples share secrets when they become intimate. Since Brandon and I were identical twins. He figured you would just start talking about your plan without you knowing I was actually Danny, not Brandon."

The Elevator doors open, ten fully geared F.B.I. agents dressed in SWAT gear exited the elevator into the penthouse surrounding Brandon Davies.

Agent Clarence Downing was the lead agent as he read the arrest warrant to Brandon.

"Brandon Davies, you are under arrest. You are, charged with one count of faking the death of your brother

Danny Davies, a second count of intent to fraud Killings Insurance, LLC out of fifty million dollars and a third count of money laundering. Please put your hands behind your back, NOW!"

The arresting agent read Brandon his Miranda rights, handcuffed him then escorted him to the elevator for a free ride to the police station.

Clarence Downing was the last man to leave after speaking briefly with Sarah thanking her for her quick thinking in a pressure situation and cooperation with the agency in bringing justice to bear against this criminal.

He then turned to Shake Danny's hand then stepped towards the elevator door. Clarence Downing pressed the button to open the elevator doors. Stepped inside and left the penthouse for the last time.

"Silence gives a person time to reflect on a recent development or life in general. It helps the mind deliberate and conclude an answer."

Danny, still standing just outside the kitchen with his hands in his pockets. He began contemplating what to say before following the same protocol as everyone else initiated. Exit the penthouse via the private elevator.

He felt he needed to say something that would give Sarah some comfort before leaving her for what he considered the last time.

"Sarah, I am terribly sorry it had to be this way. Just for the record, I developed strong feelings for you during our time together. I could not let my brother get away with this. He had no respect for you at all. He easily caved in to my request to see you without any debate or argument. My only wish is to work this out between us, if not, I will understand, I will miss you deeply. I will leave you now with your thoughts. It has been a tragic day for you."

Sarah was shell shocked by the turn of events. Still standing beside the kitchen island looking at Danny she felt in her heart he was a better man than his brother. Danny stared back with a look in his eyes that pleaded with her. Both began shedding tears.

Time seemed to stretch into infinity for Danny. He had never intended to cause Sarah such pain, and she was now acutely aware of the depth of his feelings for her.

What had initially been a misguided plan concocted by his brother that progressed into a trap to expose him.

Danny did not figure into his plan how profound his feelings of love had evolved for Sarah in such a fleeting period of time with her.

Believing it was time to make his exit, he withdrew his left hand from his pants pocket, lifted it in the air, and motioned in silence of farewell to Sarah.

Sarah, attempting to maintain a nonchalant demeanor, yearned to say something that would prevent him from leaving. Her lips pursed to form words she could not form. Just as Danny pivoted to step into the elevator, Sarah's voice reached his ears.

Sarah stopped Danny in his tracks just as he was about to step onto the elevator platform.

Hearing her words he paused.

"Danny, Please, wait!" As she volleyed one final question.

Her words hung in the air.

"Care to stay for another round?"

Dedication

I would like to take this page in this book and its writing as a dedication to my sister.

Rebecca Conaty Bruce. An accomplished author of a series of novels.

'The Esther Valentine Chronicles'

'Journey …the healer'

'Irish Bones'

The words written in this book were once in my head waiting to escape.

It was her insistence, I should pen the memory trapped in a non-existent form in my mind, transforming mere thoughts into a written version others could enjoy.

Love you Sister!

You are my inspiration.

www.ingramcontent.com/pod-product-compliance
Lightning Source LLC
Chambersburg PA
CBHW060630310726
48982CB00003B/727

9798218594961